"Throughout my reading of this collection, my unconscious played me a song by They Might Be Giants called 'Where Your Eyes Don't Go'. The tune used my skull as an echo chamber as I happily progressed through the author's clean prose and his tales of the unexpected. However, the common ground with Brandon Nolta's work is not only the band's choppy riffs; nor even the clarity of line and diction. In both artistic expressions, there is a shared recognition of that which cannot be seen — or can only be glimpsed momentarily. Indeed, in one of Nolta's stories, people themselves can disappear from the face of the earth in vast numbers. Sometimes they reappear. Meanwhile the band tells us that where your eyes don't go, a part of you is hovering… Here we are in Nolta's well-drawn galaxy of beautiful titles, believing we are safe as houses in an environment where houses are not safe; where nothing is safe; where polar extremes and the putative existence of the fantastic are no guarantee of stability either."

David Mathew, author of
Panic Soup and *The Parry and the Lunge*

these shadowed stars

Montag Press
ISBN: 978-1-940233-66-6
Design © 2020 Rick Febré

Montag Press Team:
Project Editor — Charlie Franco
Managing Director — Charlie Franco

A Montag Press Book
www.montagpress.com
Montag Press
777 Morton Street, Unit B
San Francisco CA 94129 USA

Montag Press, the burning book with the hatchet cover, the skewed word mark and the portrayal of the long-suffering fireman mascot are trademarks of Montag Press.

Printed & Digitally Originated in the United States of America
10 9 8 7 6 5 4 3 2 1

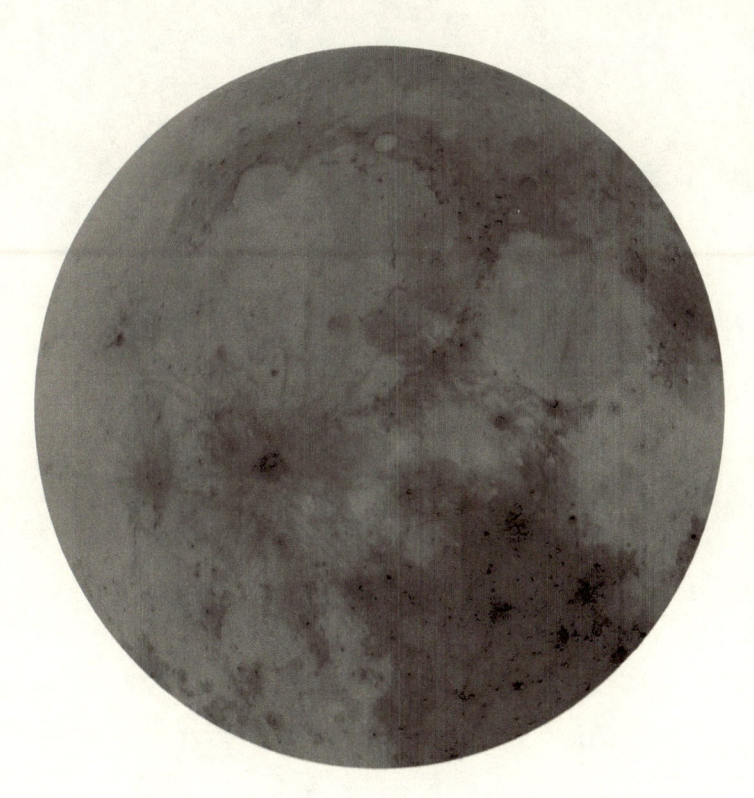

Acknowledgements

On the way to creating a book, the journey may start with the author alone, but he or she invariably—inescapably, even—accrues help along the way. Editors, people to bounce ideas off of, friends and family who drag one out of a dank writing space to see the sunlight and maybe take a shower; every book that exists had a multitude of hands moving it along. Nobody does this alone, and when a book is a collection of stories that were published in a number of different publications, the number of people who helped in some way rises precipitously. In this case, thanking them all would be a book of its own, but I'd be remiss to not hit at least the top of my particular list. Charlie and the gang at Montag Press go first, both for providing solid editorial support and being willing to take a chance with me again. Jessica Augusstson is both a longtime friend and an editor of note, whose Jayhenge Publishing provided a welcoming home to several of these stories in various collections. The good folks at Every Day Fiction have long been purveyors of thoughtful feedback and well-rounded excellence in presenting flash fiction, and I am honored that they allowed a number of these stories to make their first appearances there. Finally, as always, I'm indebted to my wife Paige, who has supported me despite my shenanigans and eccentricities for a long, long time, and thankfully shows no signs of coming to her senses.

BRANDON NOLTA

these shadowed stars

MONTAG

Table of Contents

Credits

(chronological order)

"Coffee After Midnight" originally published in *Dragon Soup* (December 1998); version that appears in this collection has been slightly re-edited.

"Voices in the Dark" originally published in *New Myths* (June 2009)

"Ecology" originally published in *The Edge of Propinquity* (October 2011); version that appears in this collection has been slightly re-edited.

"All Those Things We Never Find" originally published in *Every Day Fiction* (October 2011)

"Persistence of Memory" originally published in *Digital Science Fiction 4—Heir Apparent* (November 2011)

"Rhododaktylos Nyx" originally published in *Every Day Fiction* (February 2012); version that appears in this collection has been slightly re-edited.

"Salvation Guaranteed" originally published in *Perihelion Science Fiction* (August 2013)

"Giuseppe's Boughs" originally published in *Every Day Fiction* (August 2013)

"Many, and None" originally published in *Other Days* from Jayhenge Publishing (November 2014)

"Fire on the Night" originally published in *Encounters* from Jayhenge Publishing (June 2015)

"Elegy for a Mountain" originally published in *Selfies from the End of the World* from Mad Scientist Journal (September 2015)

"Lines in the Sky" originally published in *Every Day Fiction* (January 2016)

"Ripples" originally published in *Intrepid Horizons* from Jayhenge Publishing (April 2016)

"Memento Mori" originally published in *Stupefying Stories Showcase* (September 2016)

"The Shadow and the Rainbow" originally published in *Every Day Fiction* (December 2016)

"Back at the Cube Farm" originally published in audio format in *The Centropic Oracle* (May 2017)

"Inheritance" originally published in *Every Day Fiction* (September 2017)

"Raw Material" originally published in *Myths, Monsters, Mutations!* from Jayhenge Publishing (December 2017); version that appears in this collection has been slightly re-edited.

"The Needle and the Damage Done" originally published in *Unnerving Magazine* (April 2018); version that appears in this collection has been slightly re-edited.

"Shopping" originally published in audio format in *The Centropic Oracle* (November 2018)

For Nick and Athena

All Those Things We Never Find

For decades, everyone in town believed the house was haunted. By the time the millennium rolled around, the Calder place wasn't a house anymore, more a collection of rotted beams and jagged sheets of dirty glass, carpeted in thrown rocks and crabapples. In the 1950s, local legend claimed, Willy Calder did something horrible to his wife and children, and scampered off in the moonlight. No bodies were ever found, which was proof enough. Angela, Willy's wife and member of the town's other founding family, would never leave town on her own, so the town gossips said.

Decades saw the house grow in power over the townsfolk. Kids dared each other to spend a minute, an hour, a night inside its collapsing grandeur, steal a shred of tapestry from the sprawling library. Adults passed by in daylight, wondering when the law would get around to searching the place. Generations of sheriffs scratched their heads at the question every Halloween, the anniversary of the Calders' disappearance: why haven't the grounds and the house been searched? Every sheriff gave the same truth: nobody was officially reported missing, so there was no crime to act on, and the family trustees wouldn't allow a search without a warrant.

Official truths didn't matter. When nine kids went missing in the fall of 1967, the Calder house was the first place townspeople searched. It was still mostly standing then, the unlocked oaken doors weathered but solid. Searching from basement to attic revealed nothing, save a small handprint in the dust coating a rear window facing the woods. As the search fanned out from there, more than one in the party looked back at the

Calder house thinking of fire, but no one put torch to timbers.

Other crimes were laid at the house's front step: a trio of rapes at knifepoint in 1974, two robberies gone murderous in 1982, a homicide scored for hammer and ratchet in 1990. Children disappeared, forgotten women erased, lonely men turned the thicket around the house into a wood of suicides, and the Calder house grew in stature as it disintegrated. The end of the century came and went, but the house remained.

Fifty years of the house's existence went unmarked, not unnoticed. Markets fell, careers withered, and the Calder rot spread outward in ripples and jags, painting the town slowly in its own image. Economics trumped time, and unpaid taxes turned the Calder house into public property. Demanding truth, a great-niece of Angela Calder spearheaded a town-wide drive to search the grounds exhaustively, seeking answers to unasked questions.

More than 200 people showed up the first day, another 100 the next. Eager hands rose up against the Calder home, wall and floor and support and ceiling, shredded into ever-smaller pieces. The house was scored to its beams, scoured to the foundations and swallowed in an expanding excavation by volunteers scared by its nearness, exhilarated by its fall. Trees and thorned bushes were chopped down, trimmed to extinction.

When the search ended, the Calder house was gone, razed to a vast bare patch of dirt and stone open to the sky like a cataract, all the gnarled trees and hedges that once hemmed the Calder house devoured by long-denied tools. Across a space feared for decades, townsfolk stared at each other, bewildered at finding nothing. No bodies, no bones, no clothes or bloodied tools, no trace for cadaver dogs or ground-penetrating radar to find. Whatever crime committed in—or by—the

Calder house went with it to oblivion, and all those things the townspeople were afraid to find remained lost.

Voices in the Dark

VOICES IN THE DARK, monotones without light or inflection. I was not yet far enough from my previous assignment to know when I was still dreaming. So, the rules. Endless repetition from sun to moon.

Eschew flight, and the conveyance of animals.

It wasn't enough to be able to recite them by heart. Not to the Watched, trainers of the Keep and defenders of all within and without the faith. For their purposes and our safety, we had to know the cadence, spirit, ineffable qualities down to their molecular structure. Each rattle upon the stirrups and anvils of our ears had to invoke their weight, our lives inextricable with their rules. To be wound into that knowledge was to be among the Watched.

No shadow, no sliver of flesh or light shall pass you unnoticed.

What I remember was everywhere I turned, those rules were there, plaqued upon classroom walls, beautifully tiled into mosaic floors. Others whispered that the words could be heard in the walls and, if one ascended to the highest vantage of Forrad Hall, spelled out in the muted foliage that spotted the campus of the Keep. Only some of my fellows were joking.

Death is nothing in the Sight we guard.

But through the incessant training and recitation of rules I learned to follow as instinct, I lacked the understanding of it all. Not even the dream mills, with its great turning grottoes of luminescence and endless racks of those between, could prepare me for my new duty. The rules were part of my being, along with training in sciences and skills once thought impossible, but their purpose was not. Even as they handed me my weapons and lantern, I questioned.

Protect the Seeing, and destroy the Unwatched at every turn, for they threaten all.

"How am I of any use?" I asked, as my car was delivered. Arms full of devices, civilian clothes fitting loosely, I felt foolish, pinned by the weight of the black and white diamond badge on my lapel. The quartermaster said nothing. Silently, the vehicle I requested, an older-model Mustang meticulously rebuilt into a machine of grace, wheeled up to where we stood.

I sighed, and reached for the door. A hand on my arm stopped me, and I turned to see the quartermaster's eyes, blind pearlescent orbs through and through, fixed on mine. *The rumors are true*, I thought.

"At least you ask," he said. "Not all of you have the wit to wonder." He took his hand back, dismissing me, and motioned for the next cadet. I shuddered at his sightless dexterity, and climbed into my car, spilling items on the floorboards as I sat. Setting my jaw, I did not look back as I drove away from the Keep.

* * * * *

My first assignment was designed to introduce me to the lands where the Unwatched, among others, liked to vanish. I always thought of the Southwest as dry and harsh, inhospitable to all but the poor souls haunting the truck stops and gas stations along America's veins. Now, however, I knew better than to simply gaze along. Now I knew how to see.

To either side of the highway, an inland sea of salt flats and dry scrub spread, muted in the daylight, filled with whispers of life and promise. I could see the waiting for night rippling from the earth, spreading streamers of color and heartbeats. The mountains, stolid against the sky, loomed as if to catch my breath. Shadows stretched forth like fingers. A vault of unbroken blue perched on the mountain peaks, masking the earth from the darkness beyond gravity's reach. Such beauty. My confusion, gnawing at me since training began, abated for a moment.

I lifted my right hand from the wheel, and rested it upon the unassuming brown package on the front seat beside me, murmuring words of thanks for what I now perceived.

On the dusty gray horizon, I saw a building gradually grow into a dilapidated gas station. Its primary colors were weathered wood and rust, but other cars were parked there, and all appeared to be as it looked. The Mustang slowed as if hearing my thoughts, and I pulled up to the first pump, barely shaded by an overhead sunbreak with Esso still painted on a faded corner. No matter what else had been modified in my new vehicle, it still needed gas. I found this comforting.

A note, written on what might have once been papyrus, was taped over the gas pump's window: *Come inside*. I brushed one hand over the holstered steel in my jacket and went inside. It seemed unlikely the station person or persons were allied with the Unwatched, but not impossible.

"Afternoon," a voice rasped.

My eyes adjusted when I walked in, separating the speaker from the shadows. His form was too solid in the half-light to be Unwatched. He was an older man, solidly built, thinning blond hair under a dark blue cap, and something about him sent a shiver across my back.

"Afternoon," I said, looking at his hands. They were clean, white, almost delicate, a contrast with the black of his fingernails. A piece of training turned over in my memory, and I looked at him again, searching for a scar.

He laughed. "You won't see it, son, though you have good eyes." He motioned at his lower back. "Not unless you new ones see around corners."

"No," I said, and quickly added, "sir." Erasers, active or not, are among the greatest of the Watched, worthy of respect. Training hadn't covered the specifics of their duties, but I saw one in action as part of my apprenticeship in the mills. No nightmare is adequate to describe their duties.

"Well," he said. "Look around, but don't stay long. Traffic's pickin' up."

I nodded, and looked out the window. A small, stoop-shouldered man was cleaning the rear windshield carefully, his face thoughtful behind aviator sunglasses. The diamond on his lapel twinkled as he circumnavigated the car, shadows twinkling in his wake. He finished his task and began walking back toward the store.

I reached into my pocket to pay.

The attendant slowed, and turned his head slightly. His eyes were invisible from where I stood, but his gaze was not. It rippled in my vision like the passage of a great ship as his seeing focused on the direction from which I came.

The former Eraser turned his face toward the light. Whatever he saw was not yet there, but it was sure to come quickly. The attendant said something I couldn't hear, and headed toward a side door. What felt like a graveyard breeze passed along my neck.

"Best leave, son," a voice from the shadows said. "Worry about the road now."

I nodded, not looking toward the attendant, and headed for the door. I never believed that I would feel the Unwatched coming, chalking that rumor up to stories told to scare recruits. I now knew I was wrong. Air seemed to gather at the corners of my sight, magnifying the light. Colors became sharper. Shadows grew more defined.

In all seeing is beauty, even in the corruption we fight. Mark it all.

I reached inside my jacket and undid the clasp to the holster. Before weapons training, I had never felt the need for a gun. Now it was a thing of comfort, though it wouldn't do me much good against an Unwatched. There are other weapons that can hurt them, or even kill them if used correctly. Still, not everything on the road is Unwatched, and some things can be dissuaded with lead and gunpowder.

"Not your duty to fight here," the attendant said as he opened the door. "Drive on."

"Sir," I said, and climbed into my car. The package was still on the front seat; how stupid to leave it unguarded! Had my instructors seen this, a beating would have been the least of my worries. I placed my hand on the package, and pulled out of the station, spinning tails of red dust into the air.

The map was clear on little except one thing: there was hours of road between here and Railhead, my destination. Wide spaces on paper, little ink to mark life or civilization. Those assigned to desert runs were commanded to keep their eyes open, precisely because there appeared to be so little to see.

Dispel illusions; always see what is, not what you expect or believe to be right.

"Rules, rules," I muttered, and felt a touch of that something along my shoulders again. I looked in the rearview, and saw still nothing but the horizon and the gas station, fading as I drove my invaluable cargo away. The speedometer needle quivered at 65, rumbling in time with the Mustang's monstrous V8. *No reason to hold back*, I decided, and pressed down on the accelerator, letting slip the Mustang's engine.

The night unfurled. Twilight faded within minutes, leaving the sky to the dark and her stellar children, scattered and brilliant overhead. I glanced up to note the constellations as I had been taught: Orion, Ursa Minor, Cassiopeia. All were in their places. *Many eyes are on them*, I thought, and allowed the Seeing to fill my vision. Arcs of deep light shimmered, jagged peaks of rarer elements dancing among spectral peaks like heat lightning along a canyon. Iron and argon radiance dominated, although a rare bend in the highway brought a shell of gold winking through the desert black to my vision, a supernova beacon of defiance.

A ground flash drew my eyes. I looked forward, then checked my mirrors. The flash steadied and grew brighter in the rearview. I turned the mirror slightly to better focus. Headlights, brilliant and light blue, stared back. My senses focused as I repeated the Watcher's Litany without thinking:

Eyes open.
Hands ready.
Heart steady.
Weapons free.

The headlights grew larger, and the throaty roar of a large-block engine overpowered the wind's roar through my open window. The stars shone, keeping their secrets safe.

The weight on my shoulders spread down my back, chilling my skin. I prepared my weapons, one hand on the package. The reality of it, solid and prosaic, was soothing. I slipped it inside my coat, where it lay against my chest, warm like a second heart. An ordinary miracle wrapped in paper, no better or different than the hundreds already making their way to myriad elsewheres, yet valuable enough to draw the Unwatched at all turns. I couldn't help smiling.

Too quickly, the car pulled near. Under the wind and

engine roar, I heard another sound, soft and high like the scuttling of scorpions. A new sound, but I knew what it was. Unwatched. Darkness that walks, uncaring whether it or they lived or died, as long as a piece, any piece, of the Seeing was lost. The warmth of the brown paper-wrapped package near my heart steadied me. I took my eyes from the road ahead and looked at them.

They rode in a solid car, an Oldsmobile from before I was born, low-slung and predatory, the thunder of its passage deafening through the highway wind. I couldn't see in the back windows, but I didn't need to. The passenger window was down.

It would try to pass for female in the light. Maybe it would work; the long hair whipping from its head looked real enough, and even with the large sunglasses hiding its eyes, it had a feminine face. Perhaps it would be considered pretty to normal eyes. But there was no mistaking the malice in the grin, or the .357 in its hand. It took magic to kill an Unwatched, potent and difficult, but all it took for me was lead. I, like all the other riders on the veins of the world, am only human. The Seeing is pointless otherwise.

It smiled, its finger tightening as I watched, and I realized the thing was not wearing sunglasses.

"Filth," I said into the wind, and drew my gun at the same instant I stood on the brakes. The four-piston assembly seized the road, and I squeezed off a triad as deceleration pushed me forward, leading the shot as I was taught. The smile twisted into a snarl, and a single round winged its way into the night, yards safely away from me. The rear windshield was marred with white fracture lines and three holes near its center, but it held. My foot slammed down, and the Mustang lunged forward.

I pulled to within a car length and holstered my handgun.

Other, stronger weapons were needed. I swerved directly behind them, said a brief incantation, and pulled the gray lever under the dashboard.

The Unwatched must live mostly in darkness, shadows, murk. Light and the Seeing are their greatest enemies, and our best weapons. What the light bar was rated in human terms, I do not know. What I do know is that the Oldsmobile and its occupants were instantly the center of a Seeing, forged by processes beyond my understanding to render a terrible brilliance of focus. The universe seemed to bend in incandescent attention to the Unwatched. Stars held fast in their courses, and the Unwatched became the Seen, if only for a second. I saw the darkness part, and despite the tasks at hand, I looked to see what lay beyond the veil of cessation.

Fittingly, I saw nothing.

The Unwatched screamed in the Seeing, howling an agony in a pitch no living thing could make. My teeth ached in their sockets, and I fought the urge to brake hard and let them limp away. The artificial Seeing hurt them, but they would survive. I had one option: end them, or at least make sure they could not pursue.

Confront only when you must, but never fall back when you do. Every stand holds the world in its balance.

A flick of a switch brought the passenger window down. As I pulled alongside the rumbling Olds, I said a couplet for strength. My chest seemed to hum in time with the wind.

The driver turned to face me. Through the tinted window, nothingness sparkled.

In my hand, I held a pneumatic cylinder. I didn't remember pulling it from my pocket, but it was what I sought. Holding it outward, finger hovering over the wine-red trigger, I spun the steering wheel savagely to the right. Metal collided in a grating crunch, and I pressed the trigger as the passenger fired two shots through the driver, directly at me.

The bullets passed through the driver's face, barely rippling simulated features as they shattered the glass. I dodged the first round, which was limned by the expanding ley fire from the cylinder I held. I was not as lucky with the second; it clipped my shoulder as I lunged away, spinning the wheel and slamming on the brakes to pull away from the doomed Oldsmobile, now visibly aging as the entropic field charge did its work. Pain, sharp and searing, jolted through my arm.

Before me, the Olds sputtered and roared, swerving drunkenly as metal fatigue tattooed the car's surface, cracks and dust sprouting as I watched. The Unwatched themselves would be unharmed, too close to chaos to notice a bit more. The car, however, could not survive. Drawn to heat and electromagnetism, the charge would render machines unusable within minutes, little more than shards soon after. I spared a moment to look at my arm, blood black in the starlight. My stomach rolled as I Saw within the wound. No poisons or shadowmarks, thank God.

The tires squealed as I stopped, watching the Olds' death throes about a hundred yards ahead. Quickly, one eye on the Olds, I pulled my first-aid kit from under the seat, locating a blood patch by feel. Rough and grainy, it seemed to leap from my fingers onto my wound, digging into the skin as it corked the capillaries shut, the analgesic in the fibers already dulling the burn. I touched the package in my pocket again, rolled up the passenger window and replaced the cylinder in my jacket.

A pair of shadows leaped from the Olds, now sagging like a deflated balloon. Dust, once metal and rubber, puffed from the car in their wake as they limped toward me. The light bar had hurt them; not enough, but any damage to the Unwatched lifted my spirits. Despite their limping, both seemed to be grinning, their teeth a pale and malformed reflection in the darkness. The feminine one raised the .357.

I flicked the high beams on and stomped the accelerator. Of my remaining weapons, none could do more than injure the Unwatched, and that was already done. I had been hesitant to carry greater ordnance on my first mission, as I was not comfortable with that level of power. *Stupid*, I thought as I sped toward them, leaning low in my seat. The Seeing was in danger, thanks to my fears. Shame kept me focused on the malevolent shadows.

A roar in the night. Two. The tinkle of glass slivers flying in the wake of a steel-jacketed round. Chaos sparkling as it lowered the gun, prepared to fire again. The road between us disappeared under the Mustang's tires. I flicked the headlights off.

Be always prepared for light, even in the darkness.

Before my eyes had a chance to adapt, I hit the high beams again. I knew the Unwatched did not have the ability to perceive the visual spectrum as humans do. Even if they could bear the full light of day, they would only perceive a twilight world of shapes and motion. Changes in light could confuse them, hurt them.

They looked surprised as I hit them.

I flinched as the handgun struck the windshield, adding a sliver of damage to the bullet holes and desert grime. The Mustang lurched as I drove over the semi-solid bodies, then continued to roar smoothly toward Railhead. I looked in the main rearview, saw a spread of shadow flop and shake in my passage. My eyes told me it was pained as it tried to stand. It tried to pull itself up, but fell back to the pavement.

Where was the other one?

On my left, almost past my peripheral vision's limit, a

shadow sparkled.

I ducked and pulled to the right, barely evading claws as they tore into the upholstery. Darkness filled the window as the Unwatched dragged itself toward me, trying to pull its way into the car. Part of it was caught on the car's undercarriage, stretching it like a black crepe-paper kite. It would have been funny, but if it got into the car, I was dead. Even an experienced Watcher is no match for Unwatched ferocity in close quarters.

I roared couplets and curses into the wind, striking at the Unwatched with fist and elbow. Every blow was like punching frozen smoke, the cold of outer nothingness like needles on my skin. The Unwatched hissed and screeched, trying to strike. Between its injuries and my fury, it struggled to stay solid enough to hurt me, but all it had to do was run me off the road, damage the Mustang. On foot, I could not defeat the Unwatched. Even if I could, others might come upon me before dawn. The risk was too high.

"Soon," the thing hissed, and lunged forward. Its mouth opened as it pulsed toward my neck, teeth and rage and madness. I grabbed it where there should have been a neck, swerving as I did so. My eyes flicked to the speedometer: 85 and slowly climbing. An idea sparked. I needed both hands, if just for a second.

I slammed the thing up against the window frame, reached across right-handed to hit the window switch, my left knee firmly against the wheel. Smoothly, the glass rose, pinning the thing as the motor whined for a moment and stopped. A clawed hand grabbed the top of the glass, began squeezing its way past.

Two seconds, three at most. I grabbed the steering wheel with my left hand, reached inside my coat with my right. Felt the seam where flap met paper, lifted it with my thumb.

Eyes like pools of rage focused on my throat. Nails clicked and scrabbled on glass.

The package…unwrapped itself, it seemed. Paper fell away. Potential throbbed under my fingers, worlds spun in my hand. I pulled it from my coat.

The hand at the window found its way in. The first lunge grazed my ear. Blood welled up, a warm spot on skin grazed by vacuum chill. A hiss of triumph filled my ears. I hoped that my half-crazed idea was right.

I let go of the steering wheel for a second, grabbed the un-wrapped package with my left hand. No time now for prayers.

Its mouth opened wide. Teeth glinted in the shadows.

In one punch, I thrust the package into its mouth, up into where its brain would have been were it human. My foot slammed on the brake, calling on friction and arrested mo-tion. My mind cleared, and I turned all my attention to the Unwatched. Its mouth closed, chilling my skin even as jagged teeth tore into me.

"Let me See you," I said, and opened my perceptions to their utmost. Within the shadows, the package responded to my Seeing.

If it hadn't had a mouthful of my arm, it would have screamed.

* * * * *

The bleeding from my smaller cuts stopped within minutes. The damage to my arm was greater; despite the disinfectant and blood patches and healing couplets, it continued to leak blood as I passed the sign welcoming me to Railhead. More troubling, the chill had not passed. I Saw no shadowmarks in my arm, but beyond that, I couldn't tell. There could be any number of monstrosities making their home in me. Watcher training had been depressingly effective in showing the Unwatched were unmatched in developing horrors for their enemies.

Under the dash, the emergency beacon clicked off. I relaxed a little; only Erasers or Medics could do that remotely. Either group was welcome. I pulled into a dirt parking lot outside a brightly lit diner, improbably named Irv's, and turned off the Mustang. The package, back inside my jacket, rested warm against me. I wondered if normal people, the everyday miracles of the world, could even see this building. I was too tired, too hurt to care.

Inside, the building was clean and well-kept. Red-topped stools lined the counter, with menus and carousels of condiments placed every couple of seats. Dark velvet and brown booths lined the walls, ending at a bubble-topped neon Wurlitzer in the corner. Brightly lit, welcoming and, except for a man sitting silently with his back to me at the nearest counter seat, empty.

"Come in, son," the man said. "Let's see your arm."

I took the seat next to him, pulled up my sleeve. He placed his weathered hand on my arm, closed his eyes. The world seemed to solidify under his attention, black fingernails drawing in the diner's soft light. Warmth began to return to my skin. My fingers tingled like they'd been asleep.

"Hmmm," he said after a minute. "No infestations, no infections. Beginner's luck."

"Yes, sir," I said.

"Inventive strategy," he continued, sipping from a cup of bitter-smelling coffee. My stomach rumbled, but discipline must be kept. I would wait until the Eraser allowed it. "You handled yourself well, despite being inadequately armed. Do not repeat this error."

I nodded. Feeling had completely returned to my arm, and pain with it. Even as the flesh reknit itself, I still felt the teeth, the cold blackness on my skin. The Eraser's eyes were on my face, searching for some sign. I bore the pain, chill giving way to heat and itching, and pulled the package from my pocket. Placing it softly on the counter, I pushed it to him, relief and jealousy passing through me as he placed it in a deep scarlet bag at his side.

A moment passed. My jaw clenched as I waited for the Eraser to speak. Suddenly, he smiled widely, showing a perfect set of shining white teeth, and motioned to the bowls of food that had appeared silently before me. "Eat. There's a bed in the back; you'll stay there tonight."

"And tomorrow?" I asked.

He smiled again, but it did not touch his eyes. "Protecting the Seeing is endless. There's plenty of infinity to claim."

I turned away to spoon hot broth and stew meat into my mouth. He was gone before I looked up again. A flat package, bulkier than the last and wrapped in butcher's paper, rested on the polished counter. My name was written on it in black, an implied question in the bold inked letters. I sipped from the bowl, savoring the heat and salty sting, and looked around at the empty diner.

I picked up my piece of infinity, slipped it into my pocket, and finished my dinner. For road food, it was good.

The Shadow and the Rainbow

THE FEATHERED SERPENT faltered as it dropped below the smog line. Thousands of vehicles covered its former hunting grounds, covering the land in metal rivers and choking clouds. As it passed over the plateau's heart, its iridescent scales faded to monoxide grey; no one saw it flutter and glide to a stop at a dilapidated church. The serpent settled in an eave, tucking in its sunlight wings and curling muscular coils beneath them. It remembered when the church was a temple, and thought the change was not for the better.

A low rumble came from a shadow in the church's small courtyard. The feathered serpent turned its head toward the sound, light grey eyes flashing. It flicked its feathers. A sharp breeze rustled the cypress branches, and as the dappled light shifted, a massive black jaguar skulked from the shadows, a yellow stripe slashing downward across its mouth. The jaguar lifted its gaze.

"Tezcatlipoca," the feathered serpent said.

"Quetzalcoatl," the jaguar replied. Cabled muscles moved slowly under rolls of fur and fat. Quetzalcoatl knew its size was just for show; if he attacked, he would do so with all his unearthly speed and grace. Being the god of war suited him.

The feathered serpent drew his wings in close, waiting for his brother to get to the reason behind his invitation. It had been centuries since last they spoke. Quetzalcoatl hadn't missed his brother, but that was no excuse to be rude.

"Haven't seen you since Xolotl passed," Tezcatlipoca growled.

"True," Quetzalcoatl said. He shifted his scaled bulk, stone dust puffing from his perch.

"And you're not curious?"

"I assume you intend to kill me, brother. Why else appear as a jaguar?"

"You must be tired of flying, then. You didn't have to come."

"I'd heard you got fat; I wanted to see," Quetzalcoatl said, his eyes narrowing. "Besides, did you forget my charge? Learning, knowledge: that's me, night wind. Curiosity isn't just for cats."

Tezcatlipoca chuckled. The ruff at his neck shook in time with his mirth.

"So serious, brother. Your *charge*, as if we still commanded the world. Have you been paying attention?"

"Jaguars are terrible listeners," Quetzalcoatl said. "Learning and knowledge are my whole raison d'etre, brother. Of course I pay attention." The feathered serpent stretched his scaly neck. "Just not to you."

"Tsk, tsk," Tezcatlipoca said. "Never sleep with anyone crazier than you, never get involved in a land war in Asia, and never anger a jaguar. You know better."

"You're no more a jaguar than I am a flying snake," Quetzalcoatl said. He knew that Tezcatlipoca was trying to get under his skin, and it was working. The thought that his brother should have been the god of mild irritation crossed his mind, a familiar sensation.

"But we are something less," Tezcatlipoca said, the rumble of his voice softening. "That is why I asked you here."

The feathered serpent raised his head, suspicious now. Only the tremor of muscles gathering betrayed Tezcatlipoca's intent, but by the time his bulk sailed through the air, a muscled coil was already unwinding. Quetzalcoatl's armored tail smashed into the god jaguar, crashing him into a ruined wall.

Under the breaking of ancient masonry, Quetzalcoatl thought he heard his brother laugh. A flap of his wings, and Quetzalcoatl was perched on the highest wall overlooking Tezcatlipoca, softly laughing as he sprawled in the rubble.

"You've proved my point, brother," Tezcatlipoca said, craning his head up to meet his brother's gaze. "Could you ever do that?"

"A bluff," Quetzalcoatl said.

"Ah, but you know better," Tezcatlipoca said. With a shrug, the jaguar got to its feet, shaking dust from its haunches. "You know better than me."

"Time catches even us," Quetzalcoatl agreed.

"Yes," Tezcatlipoca said. "So, I wish to ask a favor."

The feathered serpent listened to the painted jaguar's request, his reasoning, and despite himself, could not help but be moved. *Interesting*, he mused, *that my brother, the obsidian mirror of all creation, would see past entropy into hope. I didn't think he had it in him.*

Quetzalcoatl thought for several moments after his brother finished. In theory, what Tezcatlipoca suggested would work. In theory.

"There aren't any guarantees," the feathered serpent said.

The painted jaguar nodded. "Of course, but I believe it will work. War is many things, but above all else, it is a choice. Choices can be revoked, ignored. The drive to know, to understand, is a fundament of being. Thus, you have the stronger charge, and the more durable mission."

Quetzalcoatl nodded in return. He felt the same, though whether he was up to the change was unknown. There were many war gods, while keepers of knowledge were rarer on the vine. That, Quetzalcoatl realized, was the answer. What his brother asked frightened him, but he had to know.

"No time like now," Quetzalcoatl said.

The painted jaguar lifted his face to the sun. He said nothing, but his smile, outlined in a yellow slash, was unmistakable.

The feathered serpent launched from his perch, and dove. As he fell, the solidity of both gods' forms wavered and softened, maintaining only their shapes as they allowed their godhoods to emerge. All that they were, ancient and terrible knowledge and power and responsibility, suffused them as Quetzalcoatl spread ephemeral wings and came to rest in the light of Tezcatlipoca's being.

The boundaries of Quetzalcoatl's being wavered in and out of sight as he absorbed his brother, jags of panic flaring and fading as they merged. As the light changed, the feathered serpent felt Tezcatlipoca surface briefly.

"Is it working, brother?"

The god once named Quetzalcoatl raised its wing. Under the brilliant feathers, a velvet shadow could be seen, obsidian taking its place within the rainbow. He smiled, the corners of his mouth disappearing in a yellow slash across his scaled face.

"We continue, together," the being of feathers and fur said, and took wing into a polluted sky, rising into a light beyond metal rivers and choking clouds.

Back at the Cube Farm

"Steve," a voice whispered from the top of my cubicle.

I looked up from my project spreadsheet and nearly swallowed my gum. Jim, my former colleague, was peering down at me like a mop-headed office Kilroy. It wasn't so much that I was surprised to see Jim—he'd loved working here, and told everybody so during his two years in the Netrix Services cube farm—as I was surprised to see him without cops trying to beat him down and take him in.

"Jim?" I said. "What the hell are you doing here?"

"I quit," he said, coming around to sit at his old cube, across the aisle from me. "It wasn't for me."

"You can't quit," I said automatically. "That's your assignment."

Six months ago, the semi-annual federal employment lottery had reassigned Jim away from his project management position. The United States was late to the party in creating a fully automated employment lottery—Sweden, land of IKEA and depressing crime novels, went first—but made up for it by being the first to make it mandatory. More importantly, it was one of the only lottery systems to include every conceivable profession. Even the illegal ones.

"They can't make me be an Outlaw," Jim said, shuffling the blank papers on his desk.

"Come on, man. Do you know how many people here would give their eyeteeth to do what you do?" I told him. Hell, I was one of them. Who wouldn't want to be designated one of the few state-sanctioned criminals, with almost no penalties? Outlaw status is a legal license to be bad.

"They can keep them," Jim said. "It's not as fun as you think."

Down the aisle, I could hear the ding of the elevator, the whoosh of the doors, and what sounded like the shuffle of a bison herd on the corporate-beige carpet. I peeked around the corner, and saw a platoon of SWAT personnel, guns up and swiftly moving around the edges of the cube farm. A squat fire-plug of a man in black slacks and an FBI windbreaker stood by the elevator, whispering urgently into a walkie-talkie.

"So what did you do to draw the cops?" I whispered to Jim, who'd heard the doors open. He motioned me over to his cube with a surprisingly large, matte-black pistol. *Not everything about being an Outlaw disagrees with him*, I thought as I crossed the aisle and squatted down next to him.

"Did you know the FEA sends the Outlaw designees suggestions? Banks to rob, drug dens to hit, the occasional rich couple to terrorize and tie up?" Jim said, taking a silver detonator out of his pocket. "We can go off the reservation somewhat, as long as we don't rape or kill anybody, like we need to be told. Who would do that?"

"Just executives," I said, eying the detonator.

"I never wanted to be a criminal, but I thought it might be fun," Jim said. He turned the key on the bottom of the dead man switch, and the button lit up red. Classic design. "Instead, every day, a new list of suggestions, complete with victim lists, allowed action/insurance coverage ratios, escape routes, even press releases for big-ticket crimes. I had more freedom as a paper pusher."

I nodded, wondering how far Jim was going to take this. We all got the same brochure when we turned 18, explaining how the employment lottery worked, the number of measurements that went into every personalized job list, and the intricate web of insurance and risk assessment that protected people in every employment role. Not as free as the old days, but a lot more stable.

"Can't even go to the supermarket," Jim grumbled, adjusting his jacket. Underneath, a bandolier of what looked like white clay blocks hugged his chest. News channels had started calling him Slim Jim after he blew up a bunch of cars in downtown Boston. Well, "blew up" is a little strong; he was blowing off doors, wheels, the roof of a Buick sedan in one case. Turned out every one was parked illegally.

"So…what's the plan?" I asked him nervously. Jim was good people, but the guy I remembered didn't pack explosives and pistols. *Oh, no*, I thought. *Did I opt out of the hostage coverage plan on my insurance? The cafeteria plan sounded better at the time.*

Jim pulled back on the slide of his pistol. "Thought I'd try negotiating. Ready to be famous?"

Before I could answer, an oversized hockey puck rolled in next to us. We both turned away, but the flash lit up the cube like a giant camera. Light blasted through my eyelids, and by the time I could see and hear anything other than noise and glare, Jim was face-down on the floor, disarmed and trussed up.

"Nice job, Slim Jim; that's how a real Outlaw plays it," the FBI fireplug said as he helped pick Jim off the floor. "Let's go talk to the D.A. about that so-called resignation of yours. Maybe you'll avoid jail after all."

"Jail for trying to quit being an Outlaw?" Jim asked as the SWAT guys hustled down the aisle.

"That's a serious offense," the FBI guy said. "Think you saved your ass with this little stunt. Taking a hostage in the workplace; nobody does that anymore." They hustled Jim into the elevator, leaving the official police photographers behind to gather all the pictures for evidence and insurance.

After the police medic cleared me, and the Netrix medic certified me eligible for three days' trauma-related leave, I went home. Subway was about half-full, and on every screen and smartphone, Slim Jim's face stared out, looking pained as he was stuffed into a gray police van and driven away. I sat down, leaned back, and started thinking about my employment status. Another lottery was coming up, I was eligible for reassessment, and it sounded like there might be an opening for an Outlaw soon. Maybe I'd get lucky.

Elegy for a Mountain

MY NAME IS Brother Galant ... well, Abbot Galant, actually. Of course, "abbot" is only a title. I've held it for a decade or two, but I was a brother from the first day I donned the cassock and spoke my vows to the Mountain, and that's how I think of myself. I had a name before joining, I'm sure, but whatever it was is lost to wind and stone. Surely the Mountain knows, but as one can surely imagine, It has other things to think about just now. We have many, many things to do.

Moving an abbey is no small thing. How does one move the earth? Carved from the flesh of the Mountain itself, the abbey is one with the world, perched on the peak that Brother Quillus, with his fossils and radiocarbon charts, says once stood highest in the world. The Mountain has never mentioned this, never cared about highest or oldest. It simply is. I do not know if It would even understand if we asked about it, no matter how painstakingly we rendered our query on the Quincunx Organ.

In any case, the abbey. We cannot move the physical structures; only by Its grace did the Order dare to carve the original buildings, and what few additions have been made since. Would the Mountain allow it? By the time I became abbot and had to think of such things, there was little time to form the question. Even with the reduced character set developed over centuries and the automation built into the Quincunx, formal permission to open a conversation takes years to request.

Standing on the observation deck, the infrasonic tones of the fluted brass and steel shafts bored hundreds of feet into the rock humming in my bones, I imagine the resonance plates and strikers working in tandem, pistons and bound electrons winding the machine into one Voice. Millennia and more of effort and mechanics and craftsmanship, bound to generations of the humble in service to the Mountain. From where I stand, I see scores of my siblings, maintaining the hardware, fine-tuning and testing the instruction sets, recording data and harmonic patterns for indexing and translation. They work, unhurried but with great alacrity. Ever since the Mountain declared that the fire was on its way for our planet, third from the sun that will swell in its cradle and devour us whole—well, I think it safe to say alacrity has been the general state of working.

Of course, this isn't a new development. I have been with the Order for nearly a hundred years, and the news was many generations old when I joined, but generations for a monk are shorter than reflex for the Mountain. For this massive being of thought and stone, heat and consciousness, the fire approaches swiftly, and I believe It fears for us. As individuals, we are but dust motes, but the abbey has persevered for untold eons, and It seems to value that. We speak to the Mountain and thus keep It from loneliness, or so I've come to believe.

Sister Kliendi approaches quietly as I stand at the brass railing, looking into the Quincunx heart without seeing. She steps carefully, purposefully, without the odd shuffling the Thrianx can't seem to shake no matter how long any of them try. So unlike her people, who usually thrash about as they likely did in the ancient seas from which they rose. A hint of iridescence catches my eye, and I turn to face her. The slash of scale above her eyes glitters in the light.

"Abbot," she says, bowing slightly, "we have the latest reports in from Fourthworld. The air-makers have been repaired, and the habitat should be fully reestablished well within evacuation schedules." She hands me a list of stations and other abbeys around the world, fellow seekers who have agreed to help with departing, or traded knowledge for knowledge. This world once held untold numbers and there are still many, even as twilight approaches. Our abbey will not be alone on Fourthworld.

"Fine news, Sister," I tell her, impressed by her efficiency. I remind myself to make a note in the Abbot's Journal that future project management should generally be done by those who spent at least a decade in the Archives on purpose. Those personalities are perfect for large-scale management, should the need to move a god arise again. "Has the Mountain signaled for us to begin the birthing?"

"We're receiving a signal now, Abbot. Should be complete in another decade; the Mountain seems to be in a hurry."

"Aren't we, Sister?" I ask, smiling to soften the rebuke I do not intend but she might hear. A run of chromatic notes, pinks and blues and a watery reddish-brown, plays across her face. Having seen it before, I know she's blushing. The effect is quite lovely, and strangely soothing. A moment goes by, and I allow myself to forget the magnitude of what the abbey, under the painstaking instructions the Mountain has given us over centuries, is about to do. Then it passes, and I take up my worries again.

"If Brothers Quillus and Tacton have finished their planning, tell them to be ready for signal's end. Once confirmed, they'll begin," I tell Sister Kliendi. "Fourthworld, and our siblings already there, await the Mountain."

"Yes, Abbot," she says, and turns away. She speaks to her tablet as she goes, passing the order and the double- and triple-checked instructions to Quillus and Tacton, who in turn pass their orders along to the teams of monks training, learning, preparing the cutting tools and marking where to apply crystalline paste to the outlines of the great geode near the heart of the Mountain. Nearly ready now—grown on heat and pressure and all the Mountain's memories and knowledge—to be carefully excised from this world, carried by focused light and gravity to a new world, where an extinct volcano will awaken through the Mountain's beneficence. An infant deity, given new stone, while the progenitor faces the fire. Not many of the monks seem to think much about what that truly means.

I look into the Quincunx again as I ponder this, while my fellows in the Order practice to deliver a child god from the earth.

***

Work in the translator corps long enough, many monks claim, and one can learn to feel the changes in the tones before they happen, to anticipate the notes in the earth. Given that these tones are invariant and play for months or years on end, this claim is suspect, but every brother or sister who has worked long shifts in the bowels of the Quincunx, the translation matrices, or the receptor plates believes this. When I was a translator, I felt the same, and still do.

Thus, as I walk the long paths downward to the heart of the Quincunx, a long-unfelt sensation flits from the soles of my feet upward, passing through from stone to blood to bone: imminent change, a new tone from the Mountain. I stop for a moment, half-listening, half-searching with skin and nerve. Vibrations continue to rumble beneath me. *Foolish thing*, I think after a minute.

Now, the song of warning, the litany of geologic wisdom, stops. For the first time in decades—since before I became abbot—there is only silence from the Mountain. My legs tremble, as if I had stepped from a boat and not yet recovered my land legs. I shift to one side, regain my balance. Was this the scheduled end of communication? Where was the Quincunx in full bellow, acknowledging transmission?

"Sister Kliendi," I say to the glowing icon on my wrist. A moment of silence, then her voice enters my ear, as clear as if she were there and not several levels down and north of here. "Yes, Abbot?"

"The Mountain has stopped speaking," I say. "Where is our response, our invitation to talk further?"

A poignant sigh. "We reached partial translation of this signal recently, Abbot, and the probability of this signal being a farewell was high. Given the brevity of this last tone," here, a muffled conversation with another voice, "the probability becomes certain. The Mountain has given us permission to deliver Its infant self, and has decided no further communication is needed."

"Until when?" I say. Surely she has reported this, but with the exodus to Fourthworld, I've pushed all non-critical matters off on other personnel. With a stab of irritation, I realize most of the day-to-day responsibilities have fallen on the shoulders of Sister Kliendi. *No need to report to herself,* I think, and regret my pique.

"Ever," she says. "The Mountain has nothing more to tell us."

"Then time is indeed brief," I tell her. "Quillus and Tacton have already started, I assume." Before she can answer, I feel a change in pitch running upward from the Mountain stone into my feet. I wonder if the Mountain feels the cutting, the severing of the links, even though it happens far too quickly for stone gods to perceive.

"Preparations are ongoing, Abbot," Sister Kliendi says. She almost sounds curt, which for her is a shout of rebellion.

I suspect I have pushed her too hard, a fault I inherited with the position.

"Your work continues in excellence, Sister," I say. "Thank you, and please keep me apprised of Quillus and Tacton's progress." I sign off, and look at my hands for a moment. The weight of years rushes over me for a moment as I regard the faded grey of my skin, my narrow-spanned fingers: the only sign of my true age. I am old for my people, and yet, I'm a shadow in the corner of the eye to the Mountain; blink, and gone.

I expected the work center to be nearly full with brothers and sisters, planning the disassembly and transportation of the Quincunx, looking forward to the trip outward through the blackness to the red planet, safe while our home planet burns. While the Mountain burns. However, the rows of workstations, plans and coding terminals stand empty, their usual tenders working diligently elsewhere or not at all. Surely Kliendi knows of this. I bring up the digest of notes and memos on my tablet; indeed, she does. Apparently I knew of this too, or she's learned to forge my approval sigil flawlessly. A memory stirs, and I sigh as a blizzard of administrative details in my head surface for examination.

I decide that, just for now, my advanced age is sufficient cause to rest for a moment and think of nothing, a task my earliest instructors in the Order thought suited to my nature. Old joints fold slowly, and I rest my weary back against a sparsely decorated slab cut from a species of tree extinct for more than 500 years. Another change in pitch, followed by a steady rise in intensity; the cutting has begun in earnest.

My hand brushes against the cool surface of a cavern wall, a part of the Mountain long since adapted and molded for the Order's unending work. Beneath my hand, I can sense the texture just below a surface worn smooth by generations dead long before me, brothers and sisters whose names exist only in the oldest of the Archive volumes, if at all. What does the Mountain feel? Surely nothing. Surely we are like atoms, forming and flashing into particle decay far faster than perception. These are old thoughts, I know, and yet, like dear friends or mortal enemies, they persist. The Mountain is nearly as old as the planet, and an entity of stone, the most patient of fundamental qualities. Its perceptions must be vaster than ours, slow as worlds.

The cutting continues below. I think of the sustained effort culminating in these hectic days, of all the Order who worked their lives through to reach a goal they would never see. A sunburst of pride, warming and breath-catching, silently fills my chest, and I offer a quick prayer of thanks to the Mountain. To be a part of this endeavor, to allow the Mountain's wisdom to outpace world's end and take root in new soil: I know no other word for it than joy, though some of my contemporaries might feel purpose to be a better term. Either way, it is a gift.

Reaching out, I touch the cavern wall again. Though we are blessed by this mission, I cannot deny a touch of sadness in my thoughts. Moving the child Mountain seed to the red planet will keep Its wisdom, and the Order, alive for ages to come, but the original Mountain will die with our home world. Its memories are copied into the child, not moved and cleaned from their original physical form. In death, Its new life will be born, but the old will be destroyed. For some time, this has bothered me, though I haven't spoken of it to anyone, not even Brother Averoth. If thoughts like this have occurred to the Mountain, It hasn't seen fit to share them.

"Are you afraid?" I whisper to the stone, certain It cannot hear me. Though we have no prohibition against it, I feel I am breaking some ancient rule by speaking this thought aloud.

Brother Averoth would tell me I'm being stupid; if we pray to the Mountain and expect It to hear us, It surely knows our thoughts, even those we don't say. His logic is, as always, impeccable, but my feelings are what they are. If I have any wisdom, it is only that I act on them slower now, and try to apply a measure of Averoth's good sense first.

"I would be afraid," I say to the Mountain.

The whine and pitch of my brethren's cutting tools rolls through the Mountain, a faint insistence against the papery skin on my fingers. It feels like nervous energy, a trembling before momentous things.

* * *

On the last night of cutting the child Mountain seed free, the Order celebrates. Why not? The actual operation took the better part of a year, and the cutting was the quickest part. Preparations that had unfolded over lifetimes had come to pass. The barbarians were finally at the gates, and as we prepared to flee, all we could register was relief. My predecessor would have probably waited until the Order's relocation to allow it, but my feeling was that the Mountain deserved to be there. Strange, but having had many weeks to meditate on the matter, I hadn't changed my mind.

"Serenity in the face of alcohol," Averoth says to me, a cup in his hand full almost to sloshing. Gentle black orbs regard me with keen kindness, a trick only Averoth seems to have mastered. "Since you're upright and apparently able to track movement, you must be sober."

"Perhaps I'm many cups ahead," I say, smiling.

"Have you learned to hold your wine?" Averoth asks. He knows better, but he cannot refuse to tease now; he would lose face among the initiates and junior Order. "Never mind; no point in spreading hot air now."

"Your promotion is assured, Averoth," I say. "No need to flatter me further."

I laugh alone. Averoth's smile is still there, but it slips a fraction. "Well, that answers my eventual question. Do you plan to announce it soon, or wait until it's too late to dissuade you?"

"Should I? This decision is mine."

"Others might wish to choose the same path," my friend of many decades says. "You haven't asked my thoughts, for example."

"One of the few delights of being abbot," I say, "is that one gets to decide who is invaluable, while not suffering under the delusion of being that way. Thus, my friend, you are irreplaceable, while I am not."

"Ah, the corruption of power," Averoth says, his mood darkening as quickly as his eyes.

"You'll see," I say. I hold out my hand to him, and after a pause, he enfolds my gray fingers in his solid grip. In the days to come, we'll have few chances to speak. This moment will have to do.

Eventually, he nods, releases me from his grasp and walks away, solid and sober. The celebration has run its course around us, and steps must be made. I wave my arms to catch attention, and soon enough, all eyes are on me. Except for a few specialized support personnel, the entirety of our Order is here, so what I tell them will be untouched by rumor.

"Siblings, we are nearly ready to journey to Fourthworld, the child Mountain in our arms. On the red dirt of our sister world, you will raise the Order anew, with this world's ancient wisdom to guide and nourish you.

"However, I will not be among you for this new chapter. After much reflection, I have decided to stay here with the Mountain, and tend to It as best I can until the end of this world's days. My reasons for this decision are many, but I feel my place is here with the Mountain, as It faces the fire. Your place is on another world, and I am grateful you will continue, protecting our accumulated knowledge for all our peoples.

"Once you have departed for the new world, Sister Kliendi will become the new abbot. Brother Averoth will become Senior Advisor to the office. Under their leadership, and the Mountain's continued grace, I expect a new era of intellect and compassion to begin. If it doesn't, Averoth is authorized to take drastic measures."

A few laughs here and there, but mostly silence. Well, I never was good at jokes.

"Thank you for your work and devotion. We will endure and thrive because of it. Now, our last preparations must begin. Please, to work."

Loyal and obedient, the brothers and sisters of the Order turn and file away, talk of tasks and checklists already beginning to fill the air. I believe Averoth was expecting different. Then again, Averoth is sometimes too iconoclastic for his own good. In times of change and uncertainty, routine and hard work does more to soothe hearts than any prayer, something my friend, for all of his logical prowess and clear thinking, never took to heart.

A beeping from my tablet draws me back from my thoughts. Without glancing, I know it's Sister—soon to be Abbot—Kliendi, wanting to discuss last-minute details, or perhaps ask me what I was thinking by naming her the next abbot. Not that she would be rude enough to come right out and question my sanity. No matter; her subtlety speaks volumes. I tap the icon to begin our latest conversation, walking out of the hall toward the observation deck.

***

Without the rumble of the Mountain or the multivoiced hum of the Quincunx to disguise them, the rumblings of the Order's departure flow down from the surface to pool around me, humming faintly through the railings as I stand at the deck. The Quincunx—now disassembled and stored in three cargo transports—is vast in its absence, only a cavern large enough for a city left behind to observe. I have already said all my goodbyes, stood at the rough-hewn landing space near the top of the now-abandoned abbey and waved farewell to the departing ships. After my siblings left, flying into the airless black, there was only cargo, none of which cared if I watched it depart.

Soon, even the ship songs fade and disappear, and I am alone with the Mountain. I walk along the hallways and the passages, only my footsteps and the Mountain's silence as company. Every few steps, it seems, I reach out and touch the stone, brush my fingers along walls worn smooth by millennia, tread floors hollowed by millions upon millions of footsteps. It feels warm to the touch, almost as if late summer had soaked through into the Mountain's heart.

I cannot prove this, but I believe the Mountain is aware of me.

***

On the fiftieth day after the Order's departure, as the light swells to crimson in the noon sky, the Mountain begins to sing.

Without the translator matrices and the massive Quincunx to render it, I have no way to know for sure what the message is, or even if there is one. Perhaps Its voice is enough, seemingly endless runs of shifting pulses, subsonic trills, archipelagos of meaning lost in a sea of thunder. This close to the Mountain's core, where all its messages begin, my eardrums should be split and my bones liquefying without the protective measures built into the observation hall. The fact I am whole and unharmed is evidence enough to convince. The Mountain knows someone is here with It, in the last moments before the fire consumes It whole.

I place my hands against the cavern wall, the empty space that held the Quincunx to my right. Its power courses into my skin, shaking me down to the molecules. I know that my fragile shell and the Mountain's ancient solidity will soon be plasma and wisp between the shock wave and the heat. Even now, a flicker of fear tremors in me. Maybe the Mountain feels it, too, but I doubt it. The Mountain knows many things, perhaps all. What greater comfort can there be than in knowing?

As the thunder rises, and the air turns to flame, all I can feel—in my hands, my skin, my heart—is joy.

Coffee After Midnight

NIGHT WHINED PAST THE coffee shop windows, an old dog too obedient to whimper loudly, but too rebellious to quietly accept the cold. Inside, a smoke-colored light shone discreetly down on the few tables, the long oak-colored bar, and the old man sitting at a side table, out of the way of both the espresso bar and the cramped restrooms. A half-depleted cup of coffee sat before the man, who rested calmly at his usual seat and stared past the creased paper on the table.

"Mr. Taduscz?" Wheeler the counterman said softly, and raised a chrome pot to shoulder height questioningly. Thick bitter aromas wafted from the pot, and Taduscz nodded. He had searched many neighborhoods before finding a place that served Hungarian blends. The counterman poured his cup full with no wasted motion and went back to his other tasks, leaving Taduscz to his silence. He was grateful for Wheeler's tactful ways; the graceful quality of leaving one alone is difficult to find in the city, any city.

Taduscz sipped from his cup, savoring the tart warmth. His coffee was the only indulgence he allowed himself in his twilight days, having grown too old to enjoy much else. Vices, like many facets of his life, had fallen to dust over the decades. He stared at his paper, a journal he still received from his homeland, but did not read the text. Lost in thought, he started as the door opened, clanging the bell stridently as a woman stepped inside the shop and smartly closed the door behind her, shutting out the eager night. A drizzling rain had started some minutes ago, judging from the drops she shook from her dark grey overcoat, which was slung over the Art Deco brass coatrack as soon as she removed it. Facing away from him, she gently shook water from her hair. *No pocketbook or purse,* Taduscz noted.

Finishing her task, she straightened up and walked to the counter. Although she was turned away from him, and the lighting was fairly subdued, Taduscz was struck with a strong sense of familiarity. *Does she live in my building?* he wondered. *Have I seen her on the street?* He frowned; his circle of acquaintances had become vanishingly small, and except for one or two of his neighbors, no women among them. Still, he was struck with a sense of knowing.

The woman spoke to Wheeler in a murmur too low for Taduscz to hear. The counterman nodded, and produced a large mug from his inexhaustible stash beneath the counter. Filling it with coffee, he pushed the mug across the bar, accepting the change as a penitent might take communion. She took a sip, and said something else to Wheeler, who smiled in return.

Taduscz was now very curious, not only because of his feeling of recognition of the woman. Although he could see Wheeler's face fairly well, he could not see the woman's at all. Only shadow met his eyes when he looked, the occasional flash of a nose or the curve of an eyebrow reassuring him that she indeed had a face. She stood in no shadow, and was not near any dead lights. Her face, seemingly cloaked in shadow, simply was not visible from his vantage point.

Mug in hand, she stepped away from the counter and turned toward the small gaggle of tables standing in the open space before the window. As she turned in his direction, Taduscz felt her gaze cross over him, pause, and return to his face like a searchlight. She walked toward his table, and with every step, he felt a sense of familiarity grow stronger. *This is absurd,* he thought. *How can I be so sure I know this woman when I can't even see her face? Crazy old man!*

She stopped, less than a yard from his seat, and motioned to the empty chair across the table from him. Pale and fine-boned like a porcelain figurine, her hand seemed to float in the air before his eyes. "May I sit with you, sir?"

Some of the recognition fled with her words. Taduscz prided himself on his fine ear for voices, and he was positive he had never heard this soft contralto before. "Certainly, madame. Do I know you? From the neighborhood, perhaps?"

Smoothing her charcoal suit, she laughed once, low and soothing. "Yes and no. We do know each other, Bodas Taduscz. We've known each other for years." She sat down, and her face came into the light from the recessed lamp set into the wall. Taduscz frowned at first, because he did not know the woman's face whatsoever. An angular chin, high cheekbones softened by the curve of her cheeks, a high brow with arching eyebrows penciled to wisps, ash-blond hair with discreet streaks of grey; she could have been any of a number of Eastern European women Taduscz had known throughout his life.

His eyes met her gaze, and the stillness in her eyes made the missing puzzle piece fall into place, sending a cold bolt of fear through him. A numbing spread around his heart, even while a detached portion of his mind chuckled dryly. *How can you be surprised, you old Romani fool? You knew she would be your companion again some day.*

"Bodas, I've caused you a shock," she said. "I'm sorry; please let me explain. This isn't what you expect."

"What could it be, then?" he said, lungs burning breathlessly, still feeling the numbness around his heart. "Surely you do not have time for a chat. You are quite busy."

"Time is relative," she replied.

Taduscz chuckled, a bitter bark in the quiet. "I suppose I

should be flattered."

"If you wish to take it that way, feel free," she said, no trace of sarcasm in her voice. "I would like to speak to you for a while, if I may. Perhaps we could discuss a sort of proposal."

"You'll excuse me if I display no enthusiasm for your idea," Taduscz replied. "All our bargains and proposals will end in the same way. Why bother?"

Taduscz suddenly turned in his chair and stared through the quiet shadows at Wheeler, who was methodically cleaning up the bar. He realized the hour had quickly grown late, and that, in fact, the shop was closed for the evening, and had been for some time. A suspicion grew in Taduscz's heart. "Does Wheeler know who you are?"

The woman looked at Taduscz for a moment and sighed, a gentle exhalation that slumped her shoulders a bit. "Not consciously. He recognizes this face because I've been here before looking like this, and he is attentive. You've noticed that he is, however, a sensitive man, and has been all his life, I believe."

Taduscz nodded. Other people would have missed it, but Bodas Taduscz was himself sensitive, though age and history had disguised the fact. The suspicion died away, leaving behind a silence that was all he had left of sorrow. Bodas looked at the man who had served him coffee these last few years, and wondered how much Wheeler understood. He seemed so serene. Maybe he understood better than Taduscz himself, perhaps an understanding not born of pogroms and forced tattoos. "How long does he have?"

"There is no set time for him, but I doubt he will see the summer. The disease within him has spread beyond the reach of everything but miracles. He only wishes for dignity. That at least I can grant him." She looked into Taduscz's eyes somberly, acknowledging the unspoken words.

"Dignity?" grated Taduscz. "How grand of you to give him that in a time which has no great lack. Where was this precious gift when my Eleyna needed it? Lying in the mud, being kicked into a broken stupor. Where were you and your mercy then?

"I saw you all around, then. Only a foolish young man, but I saw you, knew your step. Even the blind knew you were there, among the pits and the lines and the wooden buildings without signs. Between every breath in the winter, with every bite of the food they begrudgingly allowed, I could hear your teeth clacking in time with ours. I slept with your voice in my ears, and woke to your face every morning in the clouds from the ovens.

"Don't lie to me about dignity, or mercy, or any other noble quality you believe you give. I've seen you, heard your rattling bones too often to buy your lies."

The woman sat in silence, absorbing Taduscz's words. Taduscz glared at her, wondering whether she came to have conversation or if his time had truly come. She averted her eyes from his anger for a moment. Breathing in deep, she met his stare once again, and Taduscz felt his eyebrows lift in surprise. He had expected mockery and anger in her hollow gaze, but not sadness. It unnerved him.

"Bodas, please; you don't understand. You see me as some malevolent entity, taking what is not mine at whim and by force. Has it never occurred to you once that I may not rule what I do? You sit there in your misery and judge me evil, place all the hate and rage and pain you've accumulated over the years on me, and you spite me. There is so much more to things than that."

"Why should I should feel any different? Why should I welcome you, when you have taken so much?"

"Imagine I had not taken Eleyna," she said, her voice pushing Taduscz back in his chair and sloshing his tepid coffee onto the table top. "Should I have let her live in agony to suffer more punishment under the guards' bootheels? Is that what you wanted?

"You say I was all around you then, that my presence there belies any claims I may make now. It's true I was all around you there, but not just there. Do you think I wasn't at all the others as well, and on the Rhine, in the sands of North Africa, in the skies of London and the streets of Dresden? You suffered greatly, and I cannot tell you the depths of my sorrow for that, but yours was not the only sorrow.

"You hate me for what I am. Why should I not hate you for making me this way? Why shouldn't I hate all humans? You and yours invade lands you do not live on, capture your fellow man, and subject them to horrors that Dante would have refused to imagine. If I am evil, if I am not always accompanied by the noble qualities you profess to love so much, look at not just myself, but the people and events that summon me."

Taduscz blinked, unsettled, his rage dwindled to a spark but not yet gone out entirely. "So we have made you in our image, then."

"This face, anyway," she responded, sipping from her mug. "I have worn others or none at all, as is required. You never saw me when I took your Maria away."

"Yes," he agreed, softly. "I felt your touch in her hospital room, but never saw you."

"Few could say even that much," she said, leaning closer as she spoke. "People imagine they see Death in every shadow and hiding place when someone is dying, but very few are capable of actually sensing my presence at all. I told you Wheeler is a sensitive man, and so are you. I've known it for years, which is why I come with this proposition in mind."

"Tell me," Taduscz said. "I have nothing to lose by listening, I suppose."

She hesitated for a moment, and as she sat, twirling her drink in the mug slowly, Taduscz wondered what could make Death hesitate. *What could slow entropy in her tracks*, he wondered silently. The silence stretched on, and it dawned on Taduscz that she was not simply hesitating. She was nervous. Finally, his patience wore through.

"Well?" he prompted.

Death looked up from her coffee and sighed. "To put it bluntly, I'm lonely. I have been for ages. I need a companion, and I would like you to be that companion." She finished talking and gazed at him expectantly. Eleyna had given him the same look every time she told him she had purchased something at the market not on their list, the look that said "Let's hear it and get it done with." To his surprise, he found he'd missed that look.

"Why me?" he said automatically, his mind racing to understand.

"Why not?" she replied. "Few people are more familiar with Death than you, and those that are usually revel in my presence. I don't wish to spend eternity with that type of person. We have circled around each other for decades, Bodas, and you have always proved to be resilient. Frequently miserable and lonely, perhaps, but never truly been despairing."

"Not much criteria for a long-term companion," he said.

"You'd be surprised what I might consider important," she replied. "You've always been a decent man at heart, but you're a hopeful man as well. That combination is not as common as it should be."

"Flattery from you?"

"Why would I need flattery, Bodas?" she replied. "It's true.

Besides, we've been companions for decades, in all but fact. I've had to take nearly everyone important to you, I know. I'm sorry for that, and I want you to know that I would not have done so, given the choice."

"But you did so anyway," he said, tears forming at the corners of his eyes. "However sorry you felt, you took them to a place I can't reach. You did this."

"Yes, I did," Death said. "I did not kill them, but I took them away from you. I ended their pain and inflicted yours, and I am guilty of that."

"How do you expect me to forgive that, Reaper? How am I supposed to overlook this?" He wanted to say more, but then the tears came in force. For Eleyna, for Maria, for the family and friends fallen away over the years, lost to war and time and what Bodas had come to see as the grindstone of Fate, he cried, and felt the sorrow come up from the pit of his stomach into his voice. "How can I forgive you this?"

The clank of coins falling on the table reached his ears, and although his watery eyes couldn't see her, he knew she was leaving. A breath of cool air caressed his face, and she whispered, "Perhaps I was wrong in thinking you could. All I ask is that you consider it." Before he could clear his sight, she was gone, leaving nothing but the silvery ringing of the door's bells behind. Silence filled the room in her absence, slowly replaced by the sounds of the discreet Mr. Wheeler cleaning up the bar and preparing for the next day's business.

Bodas stood up slowly, feeling his way up from the chair only by sheer persistence. More than just his age was ailing him. For the first time in years, he knew the feeling of losing the breath right out of the soul, the sensation of clutching at memories and emotions like a drowning man gasping for air. For an exquisitely painful moment, he believed Death would simply take him now for refusing her. His chest contracted sharply into an icy ball.

"Mr. Taduscz? Are you all right?" Wheeler's voice, raised slightly in alarm, cut through the numbness around his heart, and he gasped in relief. *Not a heart attack*, his mind chanted incoherently, *not a heart attack. Just good, clean panic.* His breathing and heartbeat slowed, and he forced his voice to sound normal.

"Yes, Mr. Wheeler, thank you. I believe I'll be all right in just a moment. Got up a little too fast, I think." He turned to face Wheeler, and was struck by the care and concern he saw in the counterman's regard. A sensitive man, Death called him, and Bodas chided himself on not having realized the accuracy of that observation before.

"Are you sure, sir? I can have paramedics here in a few minutes if you need them."

"No, thank you. I'm quite fine now." Bodas smiled at Wheeler, then remembered what Death said. His smile turned thoughtful. "How are you, Mr. Wheeler?"

Wheeler looked surprised, which became a look of pleasant shock. Such truthfully meant concern, Bodas realized, might be almost nonexistent in this man's life. "Well, all things considered, I suppose I am actually…I'm actually doing well." The statement seemed to surprise him, but his smile confirmed it. "Yes sir, I believe I'm doing quite well."

"Really? I mean, with your…condition and all?"

Wheeler nodded, his smile toning down but firmly in place. "Even so. I've come to accept it, learned to live and deal with it. The fear is still there sometimes, but I've managed to come to terms with it as well. Death is now waiting in the antechamber as opposed to pounding on the door, and I believe that makes all the difference."

Bodas regarded the younger man's face carefully, as though

remembering it for the first time in years. *I wish I felt the same,* he thought. *After these long years, I wish I could feel the same.* He nodded a farewell to the counterman, wrapped his coat tightly around himself, and shuffled out the door into the night wind. Behind him, the door closed quietly, and if the bells hung off the door chimed a sadder note than usual, Wheeler gave no sign of hearing.

Fire on the Night

THE FIRE FELL AT sunset that first day. Jagged against the pocked moon, flames shivered high above the troposphere and descended past the ionosphere's skip. It tumbled past the planes, past the frantic radio waves, down into the shadowed lands of our homes and businesses. Here and there, ephemeral, waves of shimmering light dropped onto the oceans, over the mountains, splashing the electric sting of ozone smell everywhere.

Nobody knew what it was. None of our satellites sensed it coming. It fell anyway, onto children in Pakistan, on tourists ducking into Westminster Abbey, on the forgotten elderly in Arizona. No country was passed by; from low orbit, the ISS took photo after photo of the Earth's surface, swathed in what looked like sheets of luminescence. The fire held no grudges, played no favorites.

Roofs let the flames pass; the flames burned nothing inorganic. Only people, and then only slightly at the first touch, like a mild sunburn or a sharp slap. Trees continued to grow, cows kept on grazing; only the cats gave any sign of noticing, and even then just barely. After the initial panic, people felt free to be confused, belligerent, even worshipful.

But the fire offered no explanations. Everywhere on Earth, people sought answers, demanding explanations from scientists and leaders and gods who had nothing to say. In silence, the world burned, and was not consumed. Skies fell in sheaths of crackling light, and we watched. Waters glowed as lightfall entered the depths, fading and foundering thousands of fathoms deep.

When dawn came, the fire fell slower, as though the sun were protective of the realm. But still it came. The world rotated; the auroras borealis and australis continued unabated. From the streets and cafes and living rooms of the world, we watched, fearful of the fire. We watched, fearful it would end. Eventually, after time no one remembered to count, it stopped. We looked to the sky, and only then, as our gazes returned to the world, did we see what we had missed. Only then did we count what we first thought were losses in the smiling few cut from the world, their faces as frozen in joy as their bodies were in motion. Only then did we realize what the fire might mean, and even then, we turned out to be wrong.

Even now, weeks past the point when those who fell have risen again to tell us what they learned in their waking slumber, we do not know who, or what kind of beings, would speak in fire. Imagine the loneliness of creatures that speak only in flames flung across the night, hoping for some nibble, some slight touch of intelligence in the vast. Imagine their joy when an answer finally comes, even in a language they may never hope to understand. Even if we never meet, knowing another is out there...words fail us all.

Night is falling now.

We look to the skies, waiting for the fire to fall again.

Many, and None

IT'S EMBARRASSING NOW, but we thought it was the Rapture at first. We're not religious, but too many disappeared too quickly to be anything else, so we thought. Entire towns seemed to vanish, state-sized chunks of the Internet gone black overnight. Every night, the news got shorter, faces on the TV or the Web more drawn and frozen, like they were holding something back. Like most of those left, we kept keeping on, but it was hard. Everything got real quiet all the time.

The first wave went on for a week. Most official estimates say up to 20% of the world's people disappeared, but nobody was counting then. Some people took the panic better than others. There were riots, but not that many. Disappearances could happen anywhere, anytime. On the third day, some girl with an iPhone captured one in front of an Orange Julius. Whoever it was seemed to brighten for a fraction of a second, too fast to see well. Then, just air. The girl reported hearing a pop afterward.

In the second week after the vanishings started, people started to come back. Nobody came back too far from where they vanished; the farthest one I heard of was six miles from the vanishing point. He was lucky; his miles were horizontal. My best friend Anna's uncle reappeared about two miles over his house, according to the feds. Anna said his screams as he fell and the crash of him cratering the house could be heard all over the neighborhood. It could have been worse; he could have reappeared two miles underground. I try not to think about that.

Lots of people who reappeared didn't say much about

where they went. Some couldn't remember anything. Some said they were in a place that looked like a city in the clouds, while others thought they'd gone back in time. CNN found a couple of people who'd been on a space station, and one professional astronomer said she'd seen a sky with no familiar stars and two large, ringed planets, close enough to see in daylight. Some people were almost catatonic when they came back. There were reports of uninhabited worlds, wastelands, places that looked and smelled like Hell. A number of people came back in pieces, horrible wounds and marks from teeth that never existed here. Some just didn't come back.

By the end of the second week, my dad asked us to start writing in journals every day. He said it was to provide a record of some kind, proof we were here. "We can vanish anytime," he told us over dinner one night, "so we should be sure to leave something behind." He shrugged as he said it, like he'd been asked a question he couldn't answer. I think he hopes that if we prepare for the worst, it won't happen. So far it's worked, but it's not magic. It's just not our time. My brother's too young to keep a journal, so Mom works on it for him, but I've been writing in mine. It keeps me busy. Everyone watches less TV now, and the Internet's still patchy.

The disappearances haven't stopped, but they've slowed way down. After a month, only two or three people a day were disappearing in America, and other countries were about the same. Couple of months went by, and the news stopped reporting every new one. It's been six months since they began, and I don't remember who or when the last one was in town. We talk about it some nights at dinnertime.

Besides journaling, the vanishings gave me another hobby: collecting theories on what's happening, and why. When the Internet's working right, you can find a ton of sites talking about this idea or that. Lots of people still think God's testing us, maybe as a prelude to the Rapture. Aliens are popular, and Pentagon black ops, too. I even found one wackjob site that denies people ever disappeared.

The only idea that even sounded close was a blog post I found from a theoretical physicist with some university back East. I couldn't understand a lot of it; it was really long, with equations and subheadings, and the parts in plain English didn't make much sense, but he wrote something like every time a decision is made or a choice is available, universes spring up so all outcomes happen. These universes can't see each other ever, but if something were collapsing all these branching choices back into only one option, maybe all those universes would collapse. Maybe the shock of that collapse would pull people into other universes for a while, places where decisions went another way or never existed, but can't keep them permanently because they're not part of that universe, like conservation of energy.

I'm not sure what it means, but it feels right. Anyway, it seems less stupid than anything else. If it's true, I don't what to hope for. Is this the right universe? Will we all disappear? Nobody knows. I can't find that post again; the address comes up 404 when I try. That doesn't mean anything these days. I wish I could remember his name.

Tonight after dinner, nobody felt like playing cards or watching TV. My mom went upstairs to give my brother his bath while my dad cleaned up. They haven't made me do chores for a while. I try to keep doing them, but I hate washing dishes. Dad can keep doing those forever as far as I care. I wanted to write this all down while I was still thinking about it. Maybe I'll look back on this and laugh when I'm an adult. I hope so.

Too quiet around the house these days. We used to be louder, I'm sure. I can't even hear my family right now.

Now the light's on the fritz or something. It's so bright in he

Raw Material

IT WAS NEAR THE END of LC's fourteenth summer when her Aunt Chrys went to the family about her magic. "My power should have manifested by now," Chrys told her assorted aunts and uncles seated around Grandmama's parlor table, carved from the largest ash stump anyone ever heard about. LC was not actually in the parlor, having wisely taken a seat in the kitchen, just out of sight of the family gathering. Chrys was only three—nearly four—years older than LC, and while most things they did together, family rules were strong and clear on this point, so LC kept back, a blonde wisp of a girl hidden in the warmly cinnamon-scented kitchen.

"True," her Uncle Jefferson said to the gathering, "but it ain't a matter of power. You've got the spark, the juice in your veins. We just don't know how that spark's going to come out."

"Aren't there tests we can do?" Chrys asked, pale as her namesake flower.

"We've done 'em," Uncle Jefferson said. "They told us just what I told you."

"Look, sweetheart," LC's Grandmama Savannah said to her daughter, "this isn't a problem. Magic flows in you; we can all see it, light and strong. It doesn't matter so much, knowing how to tap it yet. That'll come. It always does."

"Says the woman who manifested hers before she could drive," Chrys said. LC heard the petulance like everyone else, but she picked up on the frustration and fear beneath, too. She could almost hear her aunt think *Why am I busted like this? This ain't correct.*

"I didn't pick it that way," Grandmama said, "just like Jefferson or Nikolai or you didn't. That's the way it works."

LC heard no malice or anger in Grandmama's words, but that didn't comfort Chrys. Everyone around the table talked for a little while longer, but LC knew real talk from shooting the breeze. Chrys was dismissed, and if anyone actually caught her listening, she would be too at the toe of a boot. Quickly, she snuck around the far corner, down the hallway, and up the stairs on the right side to avoid the creaking steps halfway up. Chrys was in her bedroom, lying face down on the bed and doing her best not to cry. LC flopped down next to her.

"You'll get your power," LC whispered to her. "Just you wait."

Chrys lifted her head from the heavy quilt. "Power I've got," Chrys said. "It's talent I lack."

"Maybe it's in your art," LC said, and as the words came out, LC knew they were true. She didn't know how her aunt's ability to build and sculpt fit into her talent yet—obviously Chrys didn't know either—but she could feel the words slide and latch into place in the air, creating a clarity around them. LC didn't think much about this because she'd always had it, but she'd recently come to believe that was her magic, or at least a part of it. The fullness of it was yet to be known, as Grandmama might say.

"Maybe," Chrys replied in a voice low and faintly edged. She laid her head back down on the quilt and didn't say a word the rest of the day.

***

Years rolled on, and as LC got older, she bloomed like the sunrise. It wasn't that she was beautiful, though she was pretty enough to be popular. Her magic—the knowing and reading of emotions and thoughts, and the subtle ways she could influence them, though she couldn't change them directly—blossomed not long after that plaintive summer, and with it came a confidence and a goodness that even her family, followers of the Mindful Way, remarked upon. Her heart always turned to helping, and the family honored her for it.

Her Aunt Chrys blossomed, too, though in a different direction. Despite the power running clear and strong in her, her talent didn't manifest the next summer, nor the one after, and eventually she stopped asking why. For a while after, the family stayed clear of the topic to keep it from eating away at Chrys any further, and instead encouraged her while she pursued the one talent she didn't doubt. From an early age, Chrys had been able to see any number of shapes within a chunk of wood or rough clump of stone, and her hands became learned in sweeping away the extra. As she grew, tall and magisterial, her talent and skill drew others, and she gained renown as someone bold, original, and lighting the frontier of her art as only a giant could. LC and her kin were proud, and if the possibility of Chrys' magic manifesting became more remote with each passing year, it didn't keep her from visiting home as often as chance allowed.

LC stayed close to home, moving only an hour's drive away, but art took Chrys to the world's metropolises, and there she stayed for years. Until one Thanksgiving, when Chrys told LC that she'd decided to come back to the home lands for good. While the men cleared the table and argued over what should go where in the dishwasher, LC looked at her aunt's face, trying to find any sign of joking.

"We'll all be glad to have you," LC said, "but why the hell would you come back home?"

"I decided it was time," Chrys said, brushing a strand of

raven black out of her face. "I'm going to move into the Grove, spruce the old place up a bit."

"I thought Grandmama left that to Uncle Jefferson," LC said.

"Well, he was the executor, but she split it between the kids," Chrys said. "Don't worry, I talked it over with him; as long as he ain't cleaning that big-ass house, he's cool with it."

LC shivered. "I don't know why you'd want to live there anyway. Damn spooky."

"That's part of it," Chrys said. "It's got atmosphere, and I plan on using it. Besides, what's so spooky about it? The family graveyard? Come on now."

"You do you, girl," LC said.

Chrys smiled. They talked of other things then, and laughed long into the evening. As LC climbed into her car for the drive home, she thought about Chrys living in the family manor, sitting empty since Grandmama passed, and wondered if Chrys thought she could kick-start her talent on family land, with generations of history soaked into the soil. Chrys hadn't mentioned her lack of magic in years, and without good reason, LC didn't see any reason to raise that thorn in her side. Chrys seemed fulfilled and lively, and LC knew that sometimes (though she wouldn't admit this to her therapist peers) it was better to leave the heart's sore places be.

***

Winter came and went, and spring moved in fast, turning warm before everything had time to finish blooming. As the end of May rolled near, days were hot and nights slow to cool. One pleasant midnight, LC's phone rang. She wanted to let it ring, go back to watching her hometown's gauzy shroud of dreams twist and flutter in the night sky, but she knew Chrys would just keep calling until she picked up. Only Chrys ever called this late.

"Hello, auntie," she said.

"I've finished," Chrys said. "Come and see."

"Finished what?" LC asked, but the connection was already broken.

LC frowned. She knew Chrys had been working on a large...something, but Chrys didn't talk about her work until it was finished and displayed. *Midnight isn't usually a good time for that, but if artists can't be eccentric,* LC thought, *the rest of us don't have a prayer.* Besides, Chrys' work was never boring. Incomprehensible sometimes, but not boring.

A text alert sounded, a few seconds of Donald Duck angrily squawking. LC picked up her phone.

Are you coming?

Guess she means now, LC thought, and sighed.

On my way, she texted, and stood up to go find her shoes.

***

Distances were deceptive in the moonlight, but LC didn't have any problem seeing the pale pillars of her aunt's work from the road. They seemed to float in the shadows, hunched between and around the trees that surrounded the family homestead. LC was impressed.

Chrys met her at the driveway, disheveled and excited, a gleam in her eye LC could pick out in the dark. Much to LC's surprise, she could sense a touch of magic in the air, like the ghost of lavender in the night. LC hadn't thought about it in a while, but she'd come to the assumption that Chrys' magic was latent, never to really emerge.

"Thanks for coming over," Chrys said.

"I figured you were coming to get me otherwise," LC said.

Chrys laughed. LC noticed that she didn't disagree.

They walked up the short rise to the front of the house, turning onto a rough stone path that jogged to the right and curved around the building's side. Following the path, the women passed by the extensive back yard and, to LC's surprise, headed up a narrower trail that ended at the family graveyard. LC hadn't been this way since her parents died, but she knew the way well. The land had been in her family since just after the Civil War, and although her extended family was healthy and numerous, the dead far outnumbered the living.

"You working in the graveyard?" LC asked.

Chrys didn't say anything, but nodded. Her smile said it all; LC recognized it from many holidays, though there was something flinty about it now.

"That would spook the hell out of me," LC said.

"I get that," Chrys said, "but as soon as I came home, I had this idea. Turned it over, tackled from all sides, couldn't make it work. I took a stroll through the graveyard one night, and it came to me, whole and shining. I laid everything out, and got to work."

"What are you going to call it?" LC said, and as she did, they topped a small rise. For a moment, her eyes could only pick out the ghostly pillars she'd seen from the road and a few newer gravestones from what looked like a sea of pale. A soft breeze blew over them, smelling of jasmine and the forest floor. One of the pillars seemed to move a little in the breeze.

"I'm open to suggestions," Chrys said.

A cloud opened to reveal the moon, and Chrys' art came a little more into focus. From where LC stood, it looked like Chrys simply painted some of the nearest trees and covered the land in sheets of alabaster fabric, blending the color to erase the boundary between the trees and the ground. As her eyes adjusted, LC could see that the whole graveyard area was sculpted into a new shape, flowing rises and spectral trees jutting into the night sky. It was eerily beautiful, and LC couldn't help but feel a shiver fall down her spine even as she admired the work.

A small, even path wound through the contours of Chrys' project, allowing LC to walk along without clambering over the pristine curves and valleys. As she passed the graves of her great-great-grandparents, she saw a willowy shape rising over the intersection of another path, like an abstraction of a tree sculpted into being. Walking by, she reached out and brushed her fingertips along its surface, expecting a smooth, cool, plastic surface. Instead, it was grainy, a little rough, and almost warm. It seemed to pulse beneath her fingers.

LC stopped, and gently placed her palm against the tree-like shape. Against her hand, it felt familiar. She knew this sensation, but couldn't place it.

"I like what you've done with the place," LC said, "but what is this stuff?"

"Well, we are in a boneyard," Chrys said.

LC laughed, but even as she did, a recognition born of meal preparation and school science projects and generations of magic clicked into place. Her laugh died in the moonlight as LC understood that Chrys wasn't joking.

Chrys held up her hands, palms facing inward. Faintly, LC could see sparks arcing between Chrys' fingertips, the afterimages of lines rippling up and down her fingers. Beneath Chrys' skin, the phalanges glowed.

"It took years to happen, and probably more years to figure out that it had happened," Chrys said. "You were right all along, LC. The magic was in my art, or at least that's where it becomes visible."

"How does it work?" LC asked. She hoped Chrys didn't notice that the question came out in LC's best therapist voice, the one she used when trying to avoid an eruption.

Chrys shrugged. "I can reshape the human body in any way I can imagine. Bone works a little better than flesh, living works a little better than dead. Once I realized what I could do, I'd found not only my magic, but my medium."

"So, all this…you didn't need a location, you needed materials," LC said.

"That too," Chrys said.

Chrys reached out and gently took LC's wrist. Power, softly humming and insistent, flowed up LC's arm into her shoulders, her torso, her bones. Around her, the night seemed to arc and brighten into an electric twilight. Her hair felt like it was standing on end, and as she turned her gaze to Chrys' face, she saw that in her aunt's case, it was true. Chrys smiled.

"More than anything, I need an audience who will appreciate what I'm trying to do," Chrys said. "And really, the best way to experience this is from the inside."

LC started to object, but her teeth had already fused together.

Lines in the Sky

NO MATTER WHO JAX asked about the old times, before his people made webs over the dead city, the answer was always similar. *Nobody knows, the old stories don't say.* Under the shrugs, a signal almost too faint to hear: *Why bother? Why ask?* Sometimes, if it were an elder once close to his parents, a weathered hand would ruffle his dust-brown hair.

Jax kept respect on his face, never pushing them away, though he wanted to shout: *Why don't you want to know?* But even Grandmother Ange, the wise and wiry leader of Jax's tribe, couldn't give him what he wanted to know, what his parents had once searched for incessantly.

"If we had the knowing, we've lost it," she said to him one sweltering evening, as the heat of his 16th summer's first day was just breaking over the shattered canyons of steel and glass.

"Hasn't anybody else ever looked?" Jax asked, stirring pigeon stew over the heat of a burnbowl. He sprinkled the first of the new season's herbs into the bubbling, breathing in the earthy tang of fresh basil. His mother's building-side greenhouse might look like a jagged wart, but it grew enough vegetables and herbs to keep pigeons and other birds worth eating.

"From other tribes, perhaps," Grandmother said. "After your parents returned empty-handed, no one else bothered. They went as far east as the river, and as far as they could go in the old webs, and found nothing."

"Did they go down?" Jax asked.

His grandmother said nothing for a moment, though the corners of her mouth dropped a fraction. She poked at the embers below the burnbowl, and said, "No one goes down.

There's nothing there for us."

Jax knew that tone, that frozen look that meant disapproval at best. Once Grandmother closed the discussion, there was nothing more to say. But nothing more to say wasn't the same as nothing more to know. While most his age were looking to the horizon, Jax was looking down, past layers of rope and cable and chain, beyond the barricades and doors and warning signs, into the dark clouds that hugged the city's surface, shrouding the old, dead world.

Of all the things Jax learned, the hardest to master was patience. Not the patience of the hunt; that was easy. Night after night, though, listening to the elders' fireside talk, he felt the burning inside, the need to know. Slowly, he learned. Taking what Grandmother taught—the ways of reading, how to live wisely in the webs—he prowled the shattered buildings, searching.

Many times, he found books, stories and texts from before the city died. Word by word, he began to understand. There had been some kind of attack, maybe the prelude to a war or the conclusion to one. Whatever weapon had been used was terrible, killing thousands upon thousands, changing its nature as it went. The city died, except for those that climbed into the sky, closing the way behind them. The survivors forgot the darkness's name, keeping their eyes high and their webs small: elevator cable, chains, ropes, and finally scavenged steel from the bridges, dotting the horizon like broken teeth.

Eventually, Jax came upon a day when he could find no more books, no more stories to scavenge from the elders. The answers he sought, Jax knew, could only come from below. Had his parents survived the web collapse of his 12th summer, Jax knew they would still be searching for truth, as he did. The time to stop planning and act had come.

Before the sun broke the horizon, Jax went to a hiding place in a shattered office building. Quickly, silently, he pulled out a pack, loaded with tools, weapons and supplies, and slung it across his back. He walked through halls carpeted in dirt and feathers and mold. Emerging on the side of the building away and down from the tribe, Jax climbed out into the web, clamped a gripper's extending reels onto a junction of cables, and began his descent.

As the sun arced high above, Jax vanished into the darkness hugging the city's surface, the descent cable taut as he climbed down. From the sunward side, faint sounds of the tribe greeting the day could be heard in the quiet. As the faint vibrations of the descent cable stopped, a shadow stiffly peeled itself free from an open window, looking down into the featureless clouds below.

"So much like them," Grandmother Ange said to herself. Over the years, she tried to keep the stories from Jax, avoid telling the ones she knew would thrill him, or at least change them to make a different point. His heart and mind were strong, but always in the center, an emptiness. The same emptiness, she knew, that drove his parents.

Maybe, she thought as she swung outward, *I should have told him what really happened.* But how could she? The remembering still hurt: a cool, glass-edged morning that promised warmth, until Jax's parents had emerged from the surface clouds, climbing upward so fast she hadn't noticed at first how misshapen they were, the growths and ridges and things best not remembered, even in passing.

How hungry they looked.

What would they have done, Ange had wondered, *had they reached the tribe? Would they have been able to explain what happened? Would they have slaughtered everyone?* Too much risk, too much threat. Before their guttural cries could wake the others, she'd acted. The pair of climbing axes she took from a marauder years ago were still sharp, and the tribe remained safe as her blood family fell.

From the sling on her back, she pulled a folding platform and deftly clamped it to a nexus of cables, including Jax's gripper cable. Here, Ange would wait for her grandson to return. His parents had returned within a day. The well-maintained axes, still gleaming, hung at her hip.

Alone, Ange waited from Jax to return from darkness, bearing whatever he'd become into the light.

Memento Mori

MAX PLUNGED THE SENSOR into the ground, waiting for the battered LED in the hilt to show if the decomp level in the grave made it worth digging up. If it was daylight, and if the cemetery management would cooperate, he or Jerry could have asked, saved themselves the trial and error. No point, though. The Diaspora Laws said they were obligated to dig up the dead and put them to use, but nowhere did they say anyone had to cooperate with them to do it.

Jerry sat at the controls of the backhoe, idly watching as Max waited for the sensor. Around them, a warm spring night settled on the graveyard. The lights of town, several miles away, banded the horizon in a muddy brown wash, obscuring the low-hanging stars.

"Anything?"

"Does it look lit?" Max said, promising himself a cig if they found a usable body.

Craving for nicotine curled around his guts like a cat, purring with desire, scratching at him occasionally. Lovely night like this, he almost couldn't feel the tumor in his alveoli, nestled among his breaths.

"It's old, takes a while to sniff out the methane and whatnot."

"Buy a new one," Jerry said, kicking at the backhoe's cockpit wall. His workboot made a thump against the cold metal. "We can afford it."

"New ones are too sensitive, pick up a worm fart and call it green," Max said. As he spoke, the LED indicator settled on red. Max sighed, and tore the long spike from the ground in one fast motion, releasing the smell of grass and thick dirt into the night. *Good for growing*, Max thought.

"With a new one, we'd be digging up every damn thing around."

"That'd be something," Jerry said, leaning back in the seat.

"Yeah," Max said.

He stepped to the next grave over, lifted the decay sensor over his head and slammed it into the dirt. A squeeze of the trigger, and the LED started to cycle as the sensors running the length of the spike drank in the odors and gases leaching through the soil from below. Max looked toward the town, just like many in the new West: far from the boneyard, and pulling away as much as possible.

"You're a lucky bastard," Jerry said abruptly, looking down at his hands.

Max didn't need to ask why. Jerry hadn't been on the job long, and probably wouldn't be much longer. Being around death was hard for most people, but ever since the Nystrom Process was perfected, being around what was next was worse. The last time Max bothered watching the news, before the launches and announced colonies took over the regular shows, he'd heard cremations were up 400%, even though they were illegal. Monster fines and prison terms weren't enough.

Thank God for cancer, Max thought.

The LED in the sensors clicked twice, and shone a traffic light green over the headstone. Max looked over at the marker, faded and dirty in the comfortable darkness. Lucinda something, dead for almost five years. Kind of pushing the expiration date for the Process, but that's what the test drops were for. Max nodded and jerked the sensor spike out.

"This one's fresh enough, Jerry. Let 'er rip."

Jerry nodded and turned on the backhoe. Unlike the sensor spike, it was a newer model, with a silent electric drive. Watching Jerry grim-facedly dig up the grave, only the whine of hydraulic arms and the soft crunch of thickly bladed sod being torn through for noise, Max realized he missed diesel engines. Sure, they were louder than hell, but they sounded like work. Honest labor should be done loudly, not quietly in the night, Max felt.

It didn't take long to reach the coffin. Jerry shut down the backhoe and jumped down from the cockpit, pry bar in hand. Max lowered himself into the ragged hole gently and took the iron bar from Jerry. Working this job had made Max something of a casket expert, and this one was an American Repose, made to look pretty and fall apart. A good kick would probably do it, but why risk breaking toes? Max leveraged the pry bar against the useless latch lock and busted the hasp out with one firm yank.

Jerry wrinkled his nose. "Need help, old timer?"

"Gah, too bad I forgot the Lysol," Max said, and lifted the lid to reveal a dried husk of a woman in a purple number that looked like a church getup, complete with stuffy hat. Except for the wrinkles, the gray skin and the musty smell of decomp, Lucinda didn't look too bad. High-quality embalming. Unlucky for her, maybe.

"If 'twere done, best 'twere done quickly," Jerry said.

"Into the breach, then," Max replied, and withdrew the test bands and a vial of live Nystroms from a pouch on his belt. He fastened the bands over the corpse's brittle wrist, marking an area of about an inch between them, and flicked them on. An icon on both bands turned green. Once the bands were synced up, the test Nystrom process wouldn't go any further than the area between them, which was good. A corpse that underwent the full process was damn near indestructible; even without the precise calibration of nanotech, synthetic cell growth and programming that was the full process, a body that got an uncontrolled hot dose tended to move around some and follow its own whims.

Max attached the vial to a wide-bore needle, and jammed into the wrist between the bands as hard as he dared. No sense in busting poor Lucinda up, but the Nystroms had to go deep to work. He squeezed the flexible end, pushing the smart fluid deep into the body, and waited. It didn't take but a couple of minutes for the telltale shine to steal up from within the arm, filling out the wrinkles and mummification, turning the skin a rich shade of near-purple, streaked through with hints of silver.

"Must not have had cancer," Max said.

Jerry, still hunched over the open grave, sighed and straightened up, stretching his back. "We have a winner, folks. Another meat sack with the right stuff."

"Yeah," Max said. The process would work, and Max knew the law. He and Jerry would put Lucinda in a bag, put the bag in their truck and drive her to the nearest intake center. They'd put in a body, and presto chango, out the other end would come a plasticine astronaut, with enough programming and sense to ride herd on a colony ship, the dead watching over the sleeping. Thousands of colonists and others with a one-way ticket away from Earth, a planet which might need the Nystrom Process itself before much longer, on their way to a planet that might be one of many new homes for humanity, or the only home, or nothing at all. From what the news said, or didn't say, someone up high was probably picking potential colony sites by throwing darts at star maps. Not that it mattered; with 11 billion people, humanity could afford to throw away people by the thousands for a good long while.

And at the wheel of every ship, a blue and silver machine,

made from nanotech and the best design anyone ever saw for an autonomous biped. *We can't design one, but we can sure as hell mass-produce it*, Max reflected.

Jerry offered a hand, and Max tossed him the hoist rope, tied to a harness that he fastened to Lucinda's coffin. Jerry tied it off, and after helping his partner out of the grave, he and Max got Lucinda and her splintered bed up into the night air. They loaded her into the work truck, and got the backhoe squared away on its trailer. The government was still paying pretty well for viable bodies, and one a night was enough to turn a profit for now. Max didn't see the need to fill his waking hours with work anymore.

The tailgate slammed, and Max stopped for a moment to stretch his back and look up into the sky. Light pollution wasn't too bad if you looked straight up; he could easily see the Milky Way, and a spattering of light points across the sky like dew on the darkness. Occasionally, the briefest flash could be seen from the orbital docks, and Max knew if he looked long enough, he might see a launch, a gasp of hard particles sleeting down as another one of the undead—impervious to radiation, temperature or boredom—dragged another boatload into the deep.

"Want a cigarette?" Max asked as he lit one of his own.

Jerry laughed. "Not one of them federal cancer sticks."

"Nah, these are bootleg Camels. Been saving them for my best tumor days," Max said. He held one out to Jerry, eyes still searching the heavens. They used to be so pretty.

Jerry took one. "How long?"

Max shrugged. Not long enough was the expected answer, but death didn't scare Max anymore.

"What happens if they find a cure before you croak?"

Max laughed, a bitter sound in the warm spring air. He

tore his eyes away from the sky and looked squarely at his partner.

"There'll be no refuge from the stars anymore," he said,
and took another drag, relishing his freedom.

Rhododaktylos Nyx

BEHOLD THE ROSE, glowing scarlet in the daylight of a shattered sky. It sits, perched on the edge of a crumbled pit, in defiance of the weather and acrid air. Nothing moves the rose but wind, nearly all other life here long since ground to dust. Without a companion besides entropy to follow it into darkness, the flower stands alone, a testament to the simplicity of annihilation.

Except for the dome.

It also rises from the wastes, its slick silicates and metal ribbons forming a hemispherical symmetry. A pearl in the eye of the oyster, the dome stands aloof in the land where all winds come to die. If the stories of the world before the dominion of the dome and the rose are known, only the ruins can say. Like those who made them, they too are becoming dust.

Inside the dome, an obelisk awakes. Programming falls into place, energies oscillate and align, worlds rearrange as exabytes of information come into play. The obelisk obeys. Quantum probabilities are calculated and set into asynchronous motion. Something cloaked in tangible melancholy disappears from future's end.

Sub rosa, of course.

***

In a lonely bar on an empty block, a stranger with chameleonic eyes sat down on a barstool. There was no one to the man's right to talk to or see his eyes, a brilliant shade of gold-flecked green that would have been noticed in any kind of light. That lack of notice suited the stranger fine. It wasn't why he came here.

To the stranger's left, another man sat two stools down. This man fit into the bar's aesthetic; he slumped forward, nursing a drink, radiating defeat like sunlight. The stranger knew this man's name, knew what was said on the letter the defeated man unfolded and refolded again and again. The stranger's records were astonishingly complete.

The defeated man, whose name was Allan, drank another swallow from his glass. The amber light of the liquid disappeared down his throat; the stranger could smell the bourbon from where he sat. The stranger knew about bourbon from his records. He wondered how it tasted, how it felt curling into the gut. He couldn't spare the time to find out.

The stranger got up from the barstool, walking toward the door. He hadn't been seated long enough for the bartender to notice him, but that was all right. The stranger took a folded piece of newspaper from his pocket and placed it on the bar next to the severance letter Allan received that afternoon. He tapped it once, taking care to meet Allan's eyes as he paused in his departure.

"Something for you," the stranger said. He nodded once, and walked away.

He was almost out the door when Allan opened the paper. The first inhalation of surprise came after the door shut completely, and by the time Allan thought to chase the stranger down, his obituary from three years in the future in his hand, there was no sign of the man with the chameleonic eyes.

***

Outside the flow of worlds, the obelisk watches time, endlessly scanning. It surfs the curling edge of existence, searching for currents, rapids, the occasional riptide. Deep in its central functions, where the stranger half-believes a *spiritus ex machina* dwells, the obelisk understands this task is of limited use. What it does not understand is despair, so it continues, long after the stranger alone would have withered into silence.

Besides, what else is there?

And then, on a day with only the toothy wind outside for company, the obelisk detects an eddy in the flow. As ordered, it pinpoints the ten-dimensional point where the eddy originated, and uploads the data to the stranger's net, centuries away. The obelisk continues to monitor duration's flow; something is happening.

Elsewhen, the stranger tends his tasks like a Buddhist monk raking a sand garden, and notes faint waves on the sands of history. Outside the dome, the rose waits for the dawn.

***

"Why?" Allan said aloud as he walked the blocks back to his third-floor apartment, where his wife waits, and a child on the way. He looked at the severance notice he'd received, his reward for years of long nights and white-hot effort. In his other hand, the obituary with his name. It couldn't be real, but it was: there was too much right, too many things that couldn't be known. Too many names of people unborn.

"Why did he give me this?" Allan asked the night again.

"Do you think it's a lie?" the stranger asked from the shadows of an empty alley.

Allan turned, seeing the shadow in the alleyway but unwilling to look further. He hadn't really noticed the man in the bar, but now, he was afraid to look. He had no idea what he might see.

"No. What I want to know is why you bothered. What am I supposed to do?"

Allan thought the stranger shrugged.

"Time has inertia, as everything does. History is a river; throw a pebble, make a ripple, but the river doesn't change course. Whatever we do is swallowed into the whole."

"Then why are you here?" Allan asked.

"At least we can throw rocks. If enough are thrown at the right time, the right place, perhaps a difference can be made." The stranger laughed once, a strangled noise that sounded far older than it should. "I have nothing left but to try."

Something moved in the shadows, and with a sigh, the stranger was gone. Allan stood at the alleyway's mouth, looking into shadows and pondering the stranger's words. He stared at the papers in his hand, thinking about their meaning. The wind fluttered, and Allan turned away from shadows, toward home. Along the way, he passed a trash basket. Upstream, a new ripple appeared that only the obelisk could see.

***

Somewhere, somewhen, there stands a dome. Alone in its vigil, it remains the only survivor of a world.

Except for the roses.

Ecology

Two taps sounded at the door. Soft, almost like leaning against the wood rather than a knock. Rafe waited, then heard another two, louder this time. He opened the door onto the well-lit hallway, a cocked .38 in his left hand. Snyder stood there, dressed in black jeans and sweatshirt, his hands open by his side. Snyder and Rafe had worked together for a couple months, which meant Rafe trusted him just enough to say hello. This bothered some of the hunters, but Snyder understood. He'd gone through a few too many partners himself.

"Have a drink," Rafe said, as he flicked a handful of droplets into the hall from the glass fishbowl by the door. The mist struck Snyder in the face, making him blink his eyes, but nothing else. Smoke and cries of pain would have earned the lead and silver rounds in Rafe's revolver.

"Thanks," Snyder said, wiping his face and walking into the second-floor apartment. Rafe had a rule about places to sleep; actually, he had several, but this rule resonated with Snyder: nothing higher than the second story, in case you have to make a quick exit out the back due to vampire, lycanthrope or some hex from various jujus. Not that Snyder had seen any of those. Nobody had seen a lycanthrope in 60 years, the magic players were all co-opted or in the ground, just about every other monster ever known was a rug somewhere and the number of vampires had, after more than three centuries of concerted, behind-the-scene effort, been seriously whittled down. Snyder thought he might live to see them extinct, a walking disease banished to the realms of myth and nightmare.

"Tonight's agenda," said Rafe, "had better include some

staking and baking. I'm losing my edge."

"You wouldn't lose your edge if you took a 40-year nap," Snyder said, looking out each of the dingy apartment's street-side windows in turn. Nothing moved on the street. This town, nothing more than a wide spot on a California highway, rolled up the sidewalks at nightfall, and here it was two hours past that.

"We got a mission, but it isn't the usual."

"I may not be interested," Rafe said, pouring a shot of whiskey and pounding it home. He'd poured one for Snyder out of habit, even though he knew it was a waste. Snyder didn't drink much; fighting history, he'd explained once. Still room for surprises, though; Snyder grabbed the shot glass before him and shotgunned it in one fast motion, slamming the glass down and looking at Rafe, who was staring at him as if he were try-ing to guess his weight.

"You will be," Snyder said. "We're rescuing someone."

"Ooh," Rafe said, his face twisted into mock surprise. "A damsel?"

"A weapon," Snyder said.

Rafe's eyes narrowed. He pulled out the metal chair from under the table, swung it around and straddled the back, lean-ing his arms on the backrest.

"How so? This guy shoot lasers from his eyes? Does he shit silver?"

Snyder laughed. "There's a detail I wouldn't want. Nah, it's something else. The boss wouldn't say exactly what, but it's something in this kid's genes, something that makes him valu-able. His parents don't have enough of whatever it is, I guess, but the kid…he's got something. Problem is, our old buddies know it, too. A few of them blew into town right after we did. I hear one or two of them been scouting around."

"Got any names?"

"Sticks, for sure. Maybe the Duke; he moved out of sight before our lookouts got a good eyeball on him."

"Not Johan, though."

Snyder sighed. "No, not Johan, not yet. You know that fucker's gone to ground somewhere deep. He's hoping his little minions will take out enough of us so he can get back to work, making more."

Rafe sat up, his arms still crossed and resting on the chair. "You know how long I've been on that bastard's tail. If we can clean him out before he starts a new nest or brings his forces back up to speed, we'll close the book on that branch of ugly."

"Let's not fuck around then," Snyder said, slapping the table. "This kid, maybe he's something special. Let's go collect his skinny little ass and find out for ourselves."

"Shit," Rafe said as he stood, "do we at least get to kill something?"

"It's a rescue mission," Snyder said, "everything could go to shit. I wouldn't want you to worry, though. Things might just go right."

"Sweet talker," Rafe said. "Let's bring some toys."

Snyder opened his jacket to show a collection of sharpened wooden stakes, a silver set of knuckles and a holstered pistol, a silver load in each round. An aerosol can was strapped to Snyder's hip, which Rafe knew was filled with a garlic and holy water combination, mixed with an anti-coagulant agent for good measure.

"How do you not clank when you walk?" Rafe asked, a smile making its way around his mouth.

"I keep all the anti-clank shit over here on my left," Snyder said.

"Well, let me grab mine," Rafe said, and slid a Bowie knife

into an inner pocket of his well-equipped jacket. Within a minute, they left the apartment and jogged down the stairs to the street. A pale yellow light dribbled from the working streetlight, casting jaundice over every door and window sill.

"Where's the car?" Rafe asked.

"Quicker to walk," Snyder said, unfolding a piece of paper from one of his pea jacket's pockets. "About three blocks over that way, where the bars fade out into houses with trees and kids' toys in the yard."

"Could've just said 'three blocks,' man," Rafe told his partner as they stepped into the darkness. His senses kicked into killer mode as the adrenaline began to flow, the same sharpening of perception he always got before taking on the night. Rafe knew no matter how keen his senses got, he'd never be a straight match for any nosferatu, not on his best day. Still, he'd fought and killed more vampires than anybody else in the field, and that wasn't even counting the other flavors of nightcrawler he'd put down over the years. He might not be vampire sharp, but he was sharp enough.

Together, the men made their way down a quiet street, flickering television lights from the cookie-cutter homes lighting the way. Soon they were standing on the sidewalk outside a house that was barely a cottage, its front a patchy yard ringed with a battered chain link fence. No lights were on in the house, no sign anyone was home. *If they were home, odds were good they weren't breathing*, Rafe thought.

"Smell that?" Snyder hissed, barely loud enough for Rafe to hear. Rafe did, a coppery stench that should have had every neighbor looking out a window to see who died. Of course they didn't. Nobody else could smell it or would admit it. The undead in any neighborhood tended to have that effect. Rafe didn't even blame people for their willful blindness anymore.

He understood it was only that blindness protecting them and their fragile worlds. Though it made him angry, he understood that blindness worked both ways. No vampire could last long in a 20th century where the inhabitants admitted the existence of undead.

"We might just be setting fires tonight," Rafe said.

"Or not," Snyder said, and leaped the short fence in a graceful bound. Rafe was surprised; he was used to going first. He scanned the area around the house for surprises, and saw what fired Snyder up: a few handfuls of earth were shifting from a spot just underneath the front porch, the freshly turned earth nearly disguised by the shadows against the foundation. Some vampires had taken to burying bloodsuckers that could go a couple of days between hunting as a kind of backup. Hunters always looked for daily places of rest; a vampire that could sit tight for a couple of days had an advantage.

Of course, the ones who popped up too soon weren't as lucky. Rafe leaped the fence and hustled across the front yard, holy water spritzer and stake at the ready. Killing the digger first would probably be loud, but it wouldn't do to go inside and leave a bloodsucker cutting off a retreat. Rafe drew the stake out and rushed the emerging vampire, whose hands were now visible above the ground, pale fingers and nails scrabbling the loose ground.

Just as Rafe reached the hole, the vampire's head broke surface, dirt and bugs falling as the vampire shook himself loose. Because of the dirt, the vampire hadn't opened his eyes yet, but Rafe figured he was about half a second from being noticed. He dropped to one knee, sliding across the dirt like he was stealing home, and drove the stake hard through the larynx, snapping the vampire's spine in two. The vampire opened his eyes then, wider than a human could, as his head flopped back and forth and his tongue rattled in his mouth. The vampire made no sound, but Rafe could read lips.

"That's a new one," Rafe said. He put the spritzer to the vampire's mouth and shot a long blast of garlic-flavored holy water down his throat, then sprayed his face and the top of his head for good measure. Rafe sprang to his feet, the vampire's face already a ruin of smoke and burnt flesh. The charred smell of something awful was already in the air. He stood, and saw Snyder land a furious drop kick on the front door. Splinters flew as the door burst open. Snyder lobbed a steel canister through the opening and whirled to the side. Rafe heard a hissing sound, a cough, then the sound of gagging and retching. A thick grey fog rolled out the front door, reaching up to Snyder's knees.

Rafe bounded onto the front porch, taking up position on the opposite side of the door.

"Tear gas?"

"My own recipe," Snyder said. "Silver particles suspended in warfarin, plus a couple more things for flavor. Great for rats and bloodsuckers."

"Very cool," Rafe said. "Cover me."

Snyder nodded. Rafe turned and rushed in, revolver pointed up. He heard Snyder slam the door right behind him, his gun covering the other half of the room. The house was dark, barely lit from the streetlights outside, but it was enough for Rafe to see two adults tied to chairs in the middle of the room, heads lolled to the side, unmoving. Snyder moved forward while Rafe covered the room, his eyes moving in step with his gun. He checked their necks quickly, shook his head at Rafe's unspoken question.

One footstep sounded in the hall, a light tap on the floor but moving fast, and both Rafe and Snyder turned in unison.

In the darkness, all Rafe could see was a blur, a long shadow that shimmered in the muddled night. Snyder's hand moved to his coat and had drawn the silver knuckles almost entirely out before the shimmer struck him, high and hard across the chest, launching him across the small living room and into the opposite wall. Rafe was already diving into a roll and fetching up against the corner closest to him. The shimmer moved toward him as he aimed.

"Shit," Rafe said as he fired, center, then right. The vampire dodged the first shot, but juked right into the other one, as Rafe figured. A cloud of blood puffed out as Rafe fired again, bracketing the shimmer. The vampire managed to dodge into both, the combined shock and silver poisoning slowing the vampire to its normal speed, resolving the shimmer into a tall, skeletal girl with short-cropped hair and corpse-pale skin. She stumbled, and snarled as she charged the last few feet.

A different revolver fired, and the vampire's face disappeared in a spray of fluid and bone. The faceless corpse collapsed, sprawling forward until it almost touched Rafe's feet. *Four silver rounds ought to do it*, Rafe thought, watching the body break down into ash and embers. On the far side of the living room, Snyder dropped his arm and leaned back against the wall, his head lolling as he fought to stay conscious.

Rafe got to his feet and rushed to his partner. Snyder was hurt, shaken, probably had a couple of bruised ribs, but he could move. Rafe got Snyder to his feet as gently as he could.

"Thanks, man."

"Got your back," Snyder said, a wheeze starting in his chest. "Ready to move?"

"Yeah," Rafe said, taking point. "Hope that kid's here and still alive."

Another sound in the hall, fainter than the last to their

gunshot-concussed ears. It could have been the wind, it could have been a dancing line of zombies; the darkness in the hall revealed nothing. Going in was a bad, bad idea: facing off against an unknown number of monsters who could see in the dark was a recipe for suicide, and sensible hunters would run away from such a situation.

"Flare," Rafe said, pulling one from his coat pocket. He popped the end and threw it into the hall as the end burst into crimson life. The flare rolled down the hall, singing the ratty carpet and tattered wallpaper, coming to a rest at the feet of a trio of vampires standing at the far end, a frightened boy trussed and gagged and balanced between the nosferatu. Rafe could see the boy's eyes, smell the sour terror sweat.

No time to think, to fear what lay ahead. Snyder slung himself into a standing position, and pulled a stake from his coat. Rafe was surprised his partner still had his silver knuckles. Between that, the stake and the revolver, Snyder was armed and ready. Stake in hand, his own revolver at the ready, Rafe charged forward, Snyder at his back, the toothed triumvirate awaiting them at hall's end.

Rafe held the revolver in his right hand, very mindful that he had only three rounds left. The speedloader in his pocket was full, but he'd never been able to get his reload time under a handful of seconds, and that was more than enough to get slaughtered in vampire time. Another stake was in his right hand, and he wondered if he had time to reach his own spritzer of nosferatu cocktail before he and Snyder got charged.

In the flarelight, the vampires' mouths looked weirdly elongated, like kids making faces in a funhouse mirror. One held the boy while the other two charged into fluid motion, and Rafe's conscious mind made one ominous note: the light wasn't playing tricks on him. Their mouths really were that wide, and really hung down that long. Then they were on them.

Snyder threw a hard jab at the one on Rafe's left, aiming his silver knuckles for the bloodsucker's eyes. It—the vampire was clearly a male, but only just—dodged Snyder's fist, and swung a backhand that could crush bone. Snyder ducked, dropping to one knee as he threw another punch, this one aimed at the vampire's knee. Rafe heard a satisfying crack and the sizzle of undead skin as the bloodsucker's knee dissolved under the combined force of Snyder and silver knuckles. The monster screamed, a keening wail cut short by a jagged stake ramming through its lower jaw. Snyder levered the lower end of the stake up with a wrenching push, and the vampire's jaw vanished in a spray of blood and bone.

Rafe's vampire was half a step behind Snyder's, giving Rafe a half-step worth of time to consider his options. The second vampire was marginally more careful; he launched a high, fast kick at Rafe, aiming high enough to hurt without leaving himself completely open. As the vampire's foot shot toward Rafe, he turned and let it skim by his chest, feeling the brush from its passage pull at his clothes. His right hand pulled up, and Rafe remembered he still held the revolver only when his trigger finger sent a silver load into the vampire's crotch. The report was deafening in the hall, almost as much as the vampire's agonized screech at the burning impact. Thrown back against the wall, the vampire clutched at himself as black blood, thick and ropy, poured onto the floor. Rafe took the spritzer from his pocket and let fly, spraying holy water and garlic into the ichorous wound between the vampire's legs, then up over his face and head. The screaming crept higher and higher as the wounded vampire sizzled and burned, thick oily smoke billowing from the vampire as he twitched. Rafe felt his gorge rise, and fired his last two rounds into the vampire's head. The screaming stopped.

Both men looked toward the end of the hall, where the last vampire stood, his hand wrapped tightly around the boy's pale throat. Rafe could almost see the pulse pound in the boy's neck, and if he could, the vampire must be close to taking a drink. Briefly, Rafe wondered if he could hit the vampire by throwing the now-empty revolver at him. Considering how fast the vampire could move, odds were good he'd just end up popping the boy in the head. Rafe returned the revolver to his pocket and turned just far enough to pick up Snyder in his peripherals. "You good?"

"Ready when you are. Hit him high?"

"If you can. Gotta get in close," Rafe said as he took a step forward. The vampire smiled, its vicious canines glittering in the flarelight. Scorch marks were spreading along the floor; *this place is probably going to catch fire before too long,* Rafe realized, and decided he didn't want to stop it, nor be around when it did.

"Let me help," Snyder said, and charged ahead, running past Rafe without warning. He was two steps past Rafe before he could react.

The next few moments seemed to slow into crystallized time, heartbeats like ticks of a slowing clock. Snyder was still a couple of feet from the bloodsucker and his hostage when his hand arced from his coat, the top removed from the spritzer. A fluid scythe glittered and shone in the air, spreading into drops and jagged shapes as it flew. Another stake was already in his left hand, the silver knuckles fitted around his right as he ran, focused on the vampire already in motion. Rafe saw the glitter of delight in the vampire's eyes.

Even as Rafe sprang after his partner, he saw the vampire toss the boy casually aside, slamming him into the wall hard enough to kick up plaster dust. In the same motion, the vampire seemed to lightly spring into the air, his back foot snapping through a short arc, heel forward. His mind already running the numbers, Rafe saw the vampire's kick was going to end in Snyder's face, and Snyder couldn't juke fast enough to avoid it. A shout began in Rafe's throat, but he knew even that would be too late.

Blink. The kick began its arc. Blink. The vampire hung suspended in the air, still rising, its foot scything forward with monstrous force. Blink. Moving with impossible speed.

Blink.

Contact.

Snyder's head vanished in a gout of blood, dark and eerie in the flickering red light of the flare. Shadows spiraled and fluttered as the vampire completed his kick, turning the hallway wall into a depraved modern art mural. The vampire spun in the air, coming to rest like a cat as Snyder's body, carried by momentum, spun into the wall and tumbled to the floor, a trail of grue marking its last passage.

Part of Rafe wanted to scream, to throw up what dinner he'd had, even as his body charged forward, drawing his Bowie knife in one hand while his other pulled at an ashen stake in his jacket folds. *Another partner lost*, a cold dark voice from deep inside him noted. *Another hunter down.*

Rafe flung his knife at the vampire's head, bringing his stake around like a sword. To Rafe's surprise, the vampire failed to completely dodge it; the blade scored his cheek as it spun past, burying itself in the wall beyond the vampire's head to the hilt. Hissing, the vampire turned and swung its fist with murderous speed, glancing off Rafe's ribs. He felt two of them snap under the near-miss, a white spike of pain shooting through his chest as he continued to charge forward.

Before Rafe could bring the stake forward, he knew he

would miss. The angle was wrong, he wasn't positioned correctly, whatever; he could feel it going south. The vampire seemed to know this too, or he was just enjoying the fight; his grin widened in the instant before impact, as if the pain was immaterial. A drop of Snyder's blood hung in the air before Rafe's eyes, mocking him.

Impact.

The shock of it slammed all the way up Rafe's arm, jittering his broken ribs into agony again, but even as the vampire fell back, he could see that his feeling was correct. Instead of plunging through the heart or head, both killing strikes for vampires, he had only managed to pin the bloodsucker's shoulder to the wall—a painful blow, but not fatal. The vampire's eyes narrowed, and a thunderclap went off against Rafe's head. Pain, mountain dense and heavy, flared along the side of his skull, and he dimly felt his jaw snap under the vampire's hand. Rafe fell backward, rolling into the wall behind him with a jangle of seared nerves and broken bones tangling together in a cacophony of lightning pain.

Don't pass out, Rafe told himself as he forced his eyes open. The world continued to spin as he made himself focus, made himself stand before the vampire could finish disassembling him into twitching, fiery agony. He put his hand against the wall to steady himself and, tongue pushing against his broken jaw as a focusing method, forced his eyes to clear. Despite its toothy pleasure in the fight, the vampire was still pinned to the wall, blood oozing from the wound around the stake and mixing with the plaster dust into a ruddy mud.

"Dead, hunter," the vampire said, his sibilant voice hurting Rafe's ears. Despite its injuries, it sounded gleeful. *Why not,* Rafe thought; *it's barely scratched. A stake through the shoulder might as well be a hangnail. I can barely get up, much less fight.*

"Give up, die quick like your friend. I promise," the vampire said, as if Rafe's thoughts were broadcast over the air. *Hell, maybe they were*, Rafe thought. Vampires had all sorts of strange abilities, though they were fragile against the weirdest things. Garlic, silver, holy water…

"Wait," Rafe wheezed. Adrenaline shot through him as he thrust a hand in his jacket pocket and pulled out the spritzer, a little more than half full. The spritzer and nozzle had been crushed under him when the vampire had knocked him down, and it clearly wouldn't fire.

"Can't spray me," the vampire laughed.

"Don't need to," Rafe said, as he popped the top off, ignoring the flare of broken ribs in his side and the ache of his jaw. Dropping the top to the floor, he upended the bottle over him, splashing the sanctified mixture down his face, his throat and the front of his clothes. In a moment, he was drenched, and smelled strongly of garlic. The bloodsucker's nose wrinkled involuntarily.

Rafe smiled.

"I just need to hold on," Rafe told the bloodsucker, and before the vampire could react, Rafe lunged and caught the vampire up in a powerful embrace, driving the air from Rafe's lungs with pain. He locked his wrists behind the vampire's back, oily smoke already stinging his eyes, and as the vampire began to howl like the damned, Rafe shut his eyes and pressed his body closer to the vampire's, willing every molecule of the sanctified weapon to attach to undead skin and annihilate every cell. A liquid heat began to build against Rafe, and it occurred to him his plan might have a serious flaw.

The vampire bucked and twitched, every piece of him madly seeking escape. Rafe could feel flesh bubbling under his grasp, bonds breaking and pieces tearing themselves apart. Every spasm brought new stabs of pain from his sides and jaw, but as the vampire slowly melted and came apart, he clenched his arms tighter, feeling jagged bone dig into his side but not caring. Even the stabbing pain in his ears failed to sway him, blood from ruptured eardrums running down his sides in a kind of benediction, the keening a hymn to the holy pain and cleansing fire.

After what seemed like a week's worth of pain, the monster's screaming trailed into an obscene gurgling, then into silence. A burst of searing heat flashed, and the vampire completely disintegrated, shredded and withered pieces raining onto the carpet. Rafe fell forward a step, and was shocked into a deep breath by the impact of the wall against his head. A weak scream escaped him as his ribs roared back into tender life, followed by a moan as his broken jaw bones grated against each other. He dropped to one knee and felt his stomach revolt as nosferatu blood soaked into his jeans, coldly bathing his knee. Only the pain kept his control intact as he forced himself to breathe deep through his nose, concentrating on his breathing to keep his dinner where it belonged. A minute passed, then two.

From the hall in front of him, a small moan sounded, almost too faint for Rafe to hear over the ringing in his ears from the vampire's death scream. He lifted his head and saw the boy, who'd been stunned from slamming into the wall, stir weakly. Carefully, feeling his ribs sob with every motion, Rafe crawled over to the boy and turned him over. The flare was sputtering, but enough crimson light filled the hall for Rafe to see the boy's eyes flutter and open. The boy's gaze was clear, fearful, but settled into a questioning look as the boy realized Rafe wasn't a vampire. Rafe started as he saw the boy's eyes glow in the flicker like a vampire's would, but with a different shade to the flecks and streaks. The boy wasn't a vampire, Rafe could see; his skin wasn't reacting to the holy water or garlic. Whatever he was, he was something new. Human, but something new all the same.

"Hey," Rafe managed to say. "Do you know how to drive?"

***

"These predator-prey relationships, they never quite work out," Johan said lightly, holding the black-clad human up over his head by the throat, a strong pulse of the carotid and jugular beating warm and ticklish under Johan's fingers. Above the struggling human, a dusty iron chandelier hung down from the vaulted ceiling, cheap light bulbs marring the effect. Outside, the warm strains of Dixieland jazz echoed through the swampy night, a Creole folk song turned into brassy virtuosity the bilge rats all the way out on Lake Pontchartrain could probably hear.

"Johan," the human managed to wheeze, "stop playing with your food. Get it over with, bastard."

"Please, Rafe," Johan said, his long face settling into a bored look, "don't insult me." Nonchalantly, he tossed Rafe aside, clearing a neglected rattan couch more than 10 feet away and fetching the black-clad man against the wall with a rib-cracking thump. A side table disintegrated under Rafe, throwing dust and cobwebs up in a cloud. "Did you think I couldn't smell the silver nitrate? The garlic compound in your blood? The anti-coagulants you popped like vitamins before you came here? Those were a bad idea, by the way; you're probably bleeding out internally."

"Give a guy credit for trying," Rafe said, lying on the floor, pain etched in his face. "You're one of the trickiest fuckers I've ever hunted."

"I'm the last one you'll hunt," Johan snarled, and suddenly he was there beside Rafe, a feral look in his iridescent eyes. Creatures like Johan only showed their true colors in darkest night, and Rafe admitted the effect was oddly beautiful. Not the exemplar of beauty he wanted as one of his last sights on Earth, but he had to take what he could get. Johan was right about the internal bleeding.

"Well, you've killed me good, Johan," Rafe said with as much cheer as he could muster. Dying wasn't so bad, and at least he wasn't going to be turned. No way could Johan drink his blood, not with all the crap he'd pumped into it. "I was hoping for the other way around."

"Did you know I'm the last of the originals?" Johan said, his hands reassuming their position around Rafe's throat. They lay there, cold on Rafe's skin, a weird familiarity Rafe was too weak to fight, though Johan's touch made his skin crawl.

"You and your hunter comrades have killed off the rest of us, and kept me on the run, too weak to create more. If you'd killed me tonight, vampires would be no more."

"What a shame," Rafe said, smiling through a ratcheting cough. Fluid was building in his chest, and Rafe realized that one of his lungs was punctured. "Here I am, just poisoned meat on the floor, and unable to do anything about it."

"It pains me to see you like this," Johan said, his fangs showing in the muddled moonlight, mottled by the dust on the window and the Spanish moss outside. Picking this Gothic monstrosity in the Ninth Ward wasn't too subtle, but even in New Orleans, who the hell would believe a vampire was living there? "Shall I kill you now, or taunt you some more and engender a false hope you might survive? Decisions, decisions."

"If you're going to talk all night, just kill me," Rafe said.

Bubbles of blood formed at the corners of his mouth, but Johan wrinkled his nose at the smell of anti-coagulants and silver nitrate, either one of which could make a vampire seriously ill or seriously dead. "In fact, kill me anyway; the idea of 1975 coming around with me dead and you still kicking makes me sick thinking about it."

Johan opened his mouth, but a whispery sound outside caught his attention. Even for nosferatu senses, it was nearly too faint to catch, but something was there. Johan felt it on his skin: a presence, a shape in the atmosphere, something too quiet to be human and too solid for anything else. A nauseating stench of silver and garlic filled the air as Rafe spat onto the floor, clouding Johan's senses. Johan gagged for a moment, but gained control.

"Johan, Johan," Rafe said, "you don't look well. I thought you were going to kill me."

The vampire looked at his would-be slayer. "What kind of trap do you think you have me in, Rafe? A house full of slayers? A giant UV lamp? Peter Cushing with an axe?"

"Something new," Rafe said. "Something we just found."

From the hall outside, a soft footstep, a light breeze brushing against entropic wood. Too soft to be human, one of those crashing, bungling bundles of meat and bone and blood that stamp and trumpet through the world like drunken elephants. It wasn't a vampire, though; Johan could sense their absence in the night, a grievous lack of other predators like him. They'd ruled the night with teeth and speed and fear, but the centuries had turned on them, and the humans had killed his kind with metallurgy and science, sheer numbers and their invulnerability to ultraviolet light.

"What have you brought me?" the vampire said to Rafe, rising to his feet.

An ancient, still-solid set of foyer doors swung wide, creaking and groaning with failing floor planks and tortured metal hinges. In the doorway stood a small, thin shadow, hidden from the mottled moonlight by the curve of the inner wall. Johan's eyes focused through the gloom to reveal...a child. A teenager, at best; probably no older than 14, a young boy in a hooded sweatshirt, jeans and canvas basketball shoes, a waif whose gaze was cool and unconcerned and focused entirely on the aged vampire looming over Rafe in the Louisiana darkness.

"A child?" Johan asked. "This is your plan, to distract me with a child?"

"Nope," Rafe said, voice thick with blood and foam now. "The plan was to distract you with me. That sound you hear is a trap swinging shut."

Johan laughed, and suddenly the child was beside him.

"Hello," the boy said, in a voice just beginning to descend into puberty. He looked up at Johan, and Johan saw an iridescence staring out from the boy's eyes, different in color from a vampire's golden hue—the boy's eyes showed sparks of blue and a brilliant, royal purple—but eerily similar otherwise. The effect was disconcerting.

"Was ist das?" Johan said.

"Yes," the boy said, and struck Johan in the solar plexus with blinding, unearthly speed. Air fled from Johan's lungs as he flew backward in an ugly sprawl, striking the wall eight feet behind with a meaty crash. His head punched through the plaster, and dragged a wide scar in the moldy, dusty remains of the wall as he came to rest on the sagging floor. Before he could shake off the impact and rise, the boy was once more beside him, appearing at arm's reach within a blink. *He moves like one of us,* Johan thought, *but he looks human. He **smells** human.*

"I am human," the boy said, and Johan understood the boy

shared his gift of surface telepathy. *Only vampires can do that,* Johan thought wildly, *and not all of them. What is this creature?* Johan kicked wildly, hoping to strike the boy, but he moved again, his movements visible but just barely, even for nosferatu reflexes.

A shadow loomed out of the dark, and Johan barely avoided the heavy chiffarobe as it hurtled at him. Despite age and neglect, the furniture was still solid and firm, and the boy's throw powered it through the wall and into an equally decayed room on the other side. Johan flowed into a crouch and leapt, his powerful legs launching him back toward Rafe, who Johan decided would die before this battle went any further.

"You know what an ecosystem is, Johan?" Rafe said. The damage to his lungs was obvious now; even in the gloom, a human could see the pink foam gathering on his mouth with every breath. No matter what happened to him, Johan realized, Rafe was not long for the world. *Small comfort,* he thought.

"You know what happens when something ascends the food chain and becomes top of the heap?"

Something heavy struck Johan in midair, driving the wind from him again and piercing him with jagged edges. The vampire howled in agony, and rolled into an armchair that collapsed under the weight. A table leg, chipped veneer and exposed splinters, jabbed into his ribs, and the pain was excruciating.

Impossibly, Rafe worked himself into a sitting position, his back pressed against the faded wallpaper as he strained against his broken ribs and the cumulative poisons he'd injected into his blood. Despite the splintered ends of bone Johan saw working their way through him, Rafe was smiling. "Nature adapts, Johan. Nature always keeps things in balance. Too many flowers, more herbivores appear. Weather gets too cold for too long, everything starts growing fur. After a while, too many vampires around, Nature starts growing vampire killers."

A grip like iron settled around Johan's neck and lifted him bodily off the floor. Johan felt himself spin as the fingers dug in tighter, constricting his narrow throat into a still smaller space. Below him, the boy's gaze was placid, unconcerned as he stared at the last of the vampires.

"It took a while," Rafe said, "but better late than never. Go ahead, son, pull his head off."

Johan screamed as the grip's pressure increased, and his last thoughts were lost in a blaze of agonized terror.

Salvation Guaranteed

THE RIGHT HONORABLE Galchorus Melan met us at the door himself. That was a surprise. Religious leaders don't become said leaders without picking up a retinue, and everybody in that gig wants to keep their bread and butter from being toast. Still, here he was, welcoming us to his inner sanctum, where only one other human had ever been. Since neither Julian nor I was the present Pontiff, it was a new experience.

"Thank you for seeing me here," Melan said, waving us toward a pair of SkyThrones before his desk with a pale green lower arm. Each chair would cost me a year's salary, and I'm not poor. "Security prefers I meet others in a controlled environment."

"I understand you've had some issues with separatists?" I said, nodding to my assistant. Julian had started taking notes as we stepped inside, but he was visibly writing now. Many people find Julian being quiet somewhat disturbing—he looks predatory and hungry at the best of times—so giving him a task helps keep people at ease. Melan wasn't people, but it worked with him, too.

"Not everyone in the Church feels comfortable with the direction we're heading," Melan said. "Too much dissent to handle internally, and my Council believes a schism is approaching."

I thought about what I could tell the Galchorus, the figurehead and sole authority of this planet's largest church. He had millions, maybe billions, of followers of various levels of loyalty, but that only buys you so much: *God speaks to many*. This was actually one of our mottos, something the marketing drones whipped up during my last bout under. One of the perks of working for Perception: state-of-the-art hibernation chambers, capable of putting a guy under for 150 years without damage. For those of us who like to see our work blossom, it's a godsend.

"Here's a preliminary analysis we've run," I said. "I've forwarded the full report, but I'd like to go over the gist of it. Julian, high points?"

Julian brought up a holographic display so the Galchorus could see the highlights, expanding a few bullet points for easy reading. "The Church mainstream still scores high in foundational scores and relative conceptual bias, but much of the recent scholarship indicates a shift in certain teleological underpinnings. Your school of thought is considered conservative and somewhat reactionary, especially given your stance on off-worlders. Of the disparate groups you indicated were worrisome in your initial contact, we've identified two that represent serious philosophical challenges, and one that presents a small but statistically significant chance of factioning."

Melan slumped in his seat. He didn't look surprised, but I'd only studied his species for a year, so I could have missed it. "Perhaps I will need your services, then. There's too much chance for violence if I do nothing."

"Fortunately, we have a couple of options to choose from," I said, motioning Julian to shut down the summary and bring up the service brochures. Time to talk the talk. "Are you looking for a reformation or a controlled schism? Or are you thinking inquisition? Given your history and current cultural norms, we have several options."

For the next 30 minutes, I laid out the options Perception offered, the timelines our initial analyses indicated and the payment plans available for the discerning theocrat in training. Building a socially and psychologically consistent belief system is an exhausting task, and takes decades to plan, implement and monitor. None of those services are cheap; planets are and have been sold for less. Still, the Galchorus had the coin, or indirectly controlled enough of it to make buying our services feasible.

After the initial credit confirmation and discussion of the Galchorus' overall vision for the faithful, Melan decided to go for a reformation. Not the showiest or simplest choice, but well within Perception's purview. I presented him with the updated contract, rewritten as we spoke by the finest contract app Perception could engineer, and we closed the deal. Melan's people never developed the handshake, so Julian and I bowed as we stood, arms folded as Melan's were, except for having two less apiece. The Galchorus escorted us to the door, we thanked him for his business and left. We didn't speak until we'd reached an environment we could control for surveillance, meaning our company quarters in the outskirts of the planetary capital.

"They never read the fine print," Julian said as he keyed in the contract and his notes to a q-ghost database. "Taking things on faith is par for the course, but come on."

"Nobody expects God on somebody else's schedule," I said. Various statistical packages were chewing on the original report, the notes we entered and the contract info. I knew what the number crunching would reveal, but decided to read the plan before saying anything. It's important to always leave room to be wrong.

Minutes passed, enough that I was starting to get hungry, before the report was compiled and ready. I skimmed the abstract, Julian reading over my shoulder, and focused on the methodology. Most of the bullet points we'd discussed with the Galchorus were there, but the first point was new. Neither of us was surprised. Try and find a faith that isn't built on at least one dead guy. Martyr or saint, it doesn't often matter which.

"How are we going to do this?" Julian asked. Best research-er I've worked with in years, but he's got a face like an open blade, so it's always easy to forget he has no background or training in wetwork.

"I'm already done," I said. "I was prepared before we left. Inert gene-coded virus with a nanotech trigger; once the signal is given, a protein gets switched around, and what was harm-less turns deadly. He was infected when I walked in. Nice thing is, the killer is pretty common. Nobody will have reason to think it was intentional."

"Jesus," Julian said.

"Not one of ours," I told him. I made a mental note to con-firm that with Betsy in the Archive later. Wouldn't want to lie.

Inheritance

SOMETHING IN THE DARKNESS moved, and Herr Bruegel awoke.

A large, rough hand stole over his mouth, stifling his cry before it could begin.

"Do not cry out, *Herr Anwalt*," a voice said. "I mean you no harm, but I will cause it if needed. Do you understand?"

The old lawyer nodded.

"*Danke*," the voice said. "Now I will introduce myself. Remember, no sound."

The hand moved away, and Bruegel caught a whiff of sulfur. The sound of chemical ignition accompanied a flare of light, and Bruegel saw his visitor's face. Although Bruegel had never seen him before, he knew who it was. The elderly lawyer clamped his teeth together to capture a scream.

"You recognize me," the visitor said, and smiled.

Bruegel nodded. He'd read Mary Shelley's book, heard the stories in the taverns.

"I apologize for this unorthodox approach, but it is necessary," the monster said. "The ravages of my existence are obvious."

"What do you want, creature?" Bruegel asked. "I live alone but for a few servants, and have little to interest you."

"To hire you," the creature said. "Your reputation in matters of estate law and inheritance precedes you. I wish to stake a claim to my father's estate."

Bruegel goggled at his midnight visitor. The temerity of such a demand!

"That you would ask such a thing, especially from someone who knew Victor Frankenstein, beggars belief."

"It is that foreknowledge I rely upon, *Herr Anwalt*. Why should I not claim his property? I am his creation; a singular offspring, alive through will and engineering, and all that remains of Victor. True, I have procured enough riches for myself and thus have little need of more, but his research and his library are invaluable, and his estate would be a refuge."

Bruegel shook his head, and surprised himself by laughing softly. "What you ask...." *Is impossible*, Bruegel thought to add, but kept his counsel. No sense antagonizing the brute, after all. *Besides*, a voice chimed from the depths of Bruegel's long study and experience of the law, *there are possibilities*. Quite a thorny legal issue, but perhaps if one...forcibly, Bruegel drew his attention back to the problem at hand, fascinating conundrums be damned.

"No, sir," the creature said, "what I demand." The creature gestured at the open window. In the moonlight, a shadow in the shape of a large trunk squatted. "Do you see that iron chest there?"

Bruegel nodded.

"I will tell you something that Shelley's whimpering prose did not capture. In his last days, Victor and Walton's crew surrounded my location as the pack ice closed around their keel. It was within my power to escape, but Frankenstein indicated on his honor that he wished to speak with me. Despite my fury, I was intrigued. So, for the last days of his life, we spoke at length, of philosophy and regret, science and darkness."

"You claimed to know Victor. Were you privy to his work? Did you learn that he discovered certain types of information—call it instinct, or racial memory—are passed down through biological processes from parent to child?"

Bruegel shook his head. Frankenstein's unholy science was of no interest.

The creature nodded. "I see. Well, through his experiments, he expanded on these processes, and discovered how to transmit individual memories and knowledge from one person to another. As we discussed and refined his ideas, we found the fundamental techniques were simple, even routine."

"Before he passed into delirium and death, Victor implanted one of my memories into his consciousness, a recollection of a particular meadow outside Geneva. All one needs is a sturdy hypodermic syringe, a detailed knowledge of the brain, and…well, no need to go further into family secrets."

The creature stood, looming impossibly tall over Bruegel's bed in the night. He turned, crossed the room in two strides, and hefted the iron trunk without effort. He placed the chest by Bruegel's bed. Sawdust and cold wafted from it.

"There is another important component I can reveal, Herr Bruegel," the creature said, "a relatively fresh donor brain. Preferably alive, but with careful application of cold and certain preservatives, even a severed head is useful for some time."

The creature sat on the chest and leaned close to Bruegel. "There are other ways to achieve my goals, but using the law to absorb Frankenstein's earthly holdings, rapprochement or not, has an elegant irony, and such elegance is far too scarce in my existence to let go. Take on this task, and I will reward you handsomely, both with funds and with a solemn vow to leave you and yours be as long as your professional discretion remains intact. I suspect you've read Shelley's book; you are thus aware I am an entity of my word."

Bruegel nodded. That much was true, even if the outcomes were less than honorable.

"And if I do not?" Bruegel asked.

The creature shrugged. "If you do not…well, I brought tools, and I am certain there is room in my own brain for new skills, and in that chest for the magnificent head upon your shoulders. However, I cannot guarantee all the knowledge I require would be available, and clearly, appearances before the court would be difficult. There are many variables, and I cannot control for them all."

Bruegel's heart pounded in his chest. The creature's eyes seemed to burn in the midnight shadows.

"I am, however, willing to try."

Bruegel took a deep breath to calm his nerves. Carefully, mindful of the possible repercussions, the elderly lawyer weighed his options. Helping the creature in any fashion was abhorrent, and even a slow death would not take long for a man of his years, Bruegel knew. On the other hand, without this midnight visit, would he have ever had such a chance again? Could there be a basis on which to stake such an extraordinary claim? Were there other options?

The elderly lawyer looked at the creature, and decided that he had to know.

Shopping

MACEO COULD FEEL Bette's eyes roll as he searched his pockets for bribe money. The tattooed Electronics warrior before them was thin, pale, and extravagantly tall, looming over Maceo. The curved silicon blades in his hands looked fragile, but sharp.

Finally, Maceo found a wad of currency in a front pocket: several Canuck bills, one or two antique euros and a single USNA $20. He handed it to the warrior, who accepted it and stamped Bette's Ultimart passport with a cobalt-blue spiked electron sigil. The warrior sheathed his blades and stood aside, ducking under lianaboo vines and fiber optic cables.

"Shop as you will," he intoned. "The Electronics tribe thanks you for your business."

"Remind me why we're not shopping online," Maceo said, pulling out a list. The Ultimart arcology, the only shopper-accessible retail space left in North America, was too dangerous for a casual visit, no matter how many agreements the new USNA government and Ultimart signed.

"My boss is requiring all us project managers have a specific model of wall display," Bette said, glancing up at the Morlocks in the HVAC gratings, "and the treaty Ultimart made with the manufacturer requires in-person purchase. Lighten up, dear."

She turned down an aisle overgrown with phosphorescent lianaboo. After a few minutes, they reached TV and Home Theater. They found the right unit quickly, and thanks to a series of recent treaties, armored shipping home was included for the rest of their new purchases, no added charge.

"Thanks," Maceo said when the Electronics tribesman at the cashier stand handed him his receipt and warranty paperwork. He pocketed the papers and turned to leave.

"Sir," the tribesman said, gesturing at a sturdy crate. "Your new wall display."

"That'll be delivered with the rest," Maceo said.

The cashier shook his head. "Delivery of those items is covered by treaty. Our agreement with the manufacturer requires that the display go with you."

Maceo sighed. He could argue, but USNA law was on Ultimart's side. That left only one real option to get out. He turned to Bette, who nodded in reply. She knew Ultimart better than he did, and understood that the rapids—fast, direct, and an unprotected free-fire zone the whole way—were their ticket home.

Quickly, a trio of tribesmen formed up around the crate. The warriors led Bette and Maceo out to a large circular expanse that merged seamlessly into a massive pillar, rapids tumbling restlessly through its center. Decades of cobbling and repair had expanded what once was a massive water slide into an indoor river, fed from rooftop tanks, catch traps, and who knew what else. Ragged notches on either side of the rapids held tethered plastic rafts. The Electronics warriors placed the crate at the water's edge, then bowed and headed back.

"Let's get our socks wet," Maceo said, and began loading the crate. They lashed it down, climbed aboard, and pushed off, letting the raft nose into the current. The steady flow pulled them into the center, several feet of clearance on either side.

The rapids ran level for several blocks past Electronics, but just past Children's, the rapids bent sharply and started downward, disappearing past Armor. As they reached the bend, Bette turned casually to Maceo and said, "Somebody's watching. Straight over Armor, two pipes to the right."

Maceo leaned back, pretending to yawn. A slash of red

was visible in the foliage, and the outline of someone crouching, outlined against the pearly artificial sky. A faint shift to the right drew his eye, and two warriors appeared, spears in hand. Shadows leaped from the foliage toward hanging vines woven loosely into ropes, which reached down to a rough platform just behind them.

"If they sneeze hard, I'm ready," Bette whispered.

"OK," Maceo said. Being ready was part of the shopping experience in a store that survived a world going to hell by facing inward, turning employees seeking safety into citizens and, eventually, their own tribes. He knew the history.

The first shadow reached the platform, a skinny woman with Arts and Crafts tattoos. A bone-colored blade sat at her hip, a bamboo short spear strapped across her back. Maceo figured she was maybe 18; the long scar from eyebrow to lip made it hard to tell. A bump in the channel lifted the raft, and the warrior's arm jerked. Bette's hand darted up her sleeve. Before the warrior could cast, Bette's throwing knife sliced a thin red mist from the warrior's ear. The warrior squawked and vanished into the foliage.

Shouts rolled from the green mottle above, and spears and chunks of old tiling rained down. A pair of shapes lunged from the canopy, swinging down toward them. Both had spears, and the taller of the two, an improbably beautiful young woman, held a neon-green blowgun to her lips.

"Honey, warning shot," Bette said, picking up her machete. Maceo hefted his pistol, took a deep breath, and let it out slowly as he squeezed the trigger. A cloud puffed from a vine, and the beautiful warrior spun wildly into her companion. Maceo thought they would fall, but the woman snagged a vine as they spun and swung them to safety. The rapids carried the raft past the curve and down into the ground levels before the warriors could catch up.

After a couple of short turns, the rapids leveled out, and Maceo saw the opening to Terminus, the vast artificial lagoon that marked the arcology's exit. They rowed toward the closest exit, marked in bright yellow LEDs. Protected by treaty and the Morlocks, it was the safest place in Ultimart. Maceo swiftly tied the raft to the ramp, trying to not think about their near misses.

"Help a lady out?" Bette laughed. Maceo nodded, and noticed the tremble in her hand as he reached for her. As a good, dutiful husband, he didn't say anything. *Hope we can stick to online shopping for a while,* Maceo thought, and began planning the safest, least gunfire-prone way home.

The Needle and the Damage Done

IN THE NIGHT OUTSIDE the city morgue, distant thunder echoes off concrete and steel. The cop on duty pulls back the sheet from the dead girl's face. My girl's face. She was pretty, once. Hard to tell now.

I look down, knowing this identification is just a formality. The corpse on the gurney was my daughter once, before endless rounds of sobriety and relapse. Before tonight, the last time I'd seen her was 10 days ago, fresh from rehab. She'd seemed lively, willing to try again. Just like before. I turn away.

The cop clearly knows no words are ever right. He tries anyway. "Dr. Tiamat, I'm very sorry."

"So am I," I whisper, not looking up. I know she can see me from the dirty sky.

**

It's all actually fairly simple. The invader floats unchallenged through the stream. Lymphocytes recognize my carefully engineered signature as that of a brother cell and let it pass. It tumbles through the aorta and into the highways of vein and artery. Slumbering in the flow, it patiently waits to reach its destination.

By design, it slips through the blood-brain barrier. A coded protein sheath dissolves, and its viral core floats free. It samples the flow for the chemical scent it was made to follow like a bloodhound.

Faintly, barely a whisper in the blood, a neurochemical trace reaches the invader. The virus tastes its quarry: an alka-

loid compound in the warmth, a breath of opiate in the roar.
All its viral dreams coming true.

**

There are many I watch as part of my testing protocol, but
this one is special. From the day's shadows, I see what used to
be a high-school track star named Dom as he waits for his man.
The man, known to him and my Juliana as Cork, is late. He
doesn't care if he's on time. Junkies wait. Thus, Dom waits, as
Juliana did.

He trembles as soon as Cork steps around the corner. Even
I, dispassionate as the dead, can see that Dom feels the fire in
his bones, the twitch and jitter in his skin. He needs it, more
than food or sex or air.

Money changes hands. A plastic bag and fresh syringe are
handed over. Rumor has it that Cork prides himself on giving
good bang for the buck, and always with a grin. Nobody else
smiles at Dom now. Dom holds back the shakes long enough
to pocket the bag and turn home. Cork fades into corduroy
shadows, gone.

**

After years of work and failure and restarts and repeating
the whole process again and again, I can picture it as if it were
unfolding before me. Adrift among the alkaloids, the virus
transforms, seeking different prey. Settling among unwary new
neighbors, it forms a crèche, which begins to bleed neurotrans-
mitters into nearby cells. Messages change. Another generation spawns, and the invaders settle to their purpose, spreading
throughout the brain. New settlements arise.

However, the new residents won't live with just any neuro-chemical that floats by; my children are choosy. Soon, the invaders block nearly all local serotonin production. The affected area is small, but the invaders are fast, and their neighborhood expands.

**

That night, how did it all unfold, I wonder? The transcripts aren't clear, and what little I could glean from Dom's brother Orange wasn't much more detailed. Did Orange hold the phone, frozen, as screaming filled the filthy hallway behind him? He claimed that Dom didn't slow down for nearly 20 minutes, as Orange waited with only tinny hold music to accompany him.

Did Orange walk down the hall to the blistered door of the apartment's single bedroom, making the sign of the cross as he did? Was the tang of copper clear from the moment he opened the door? Orange didn't tell me these things, but I like to imagine them as true.

Not that it means much from an empirical point of view, of course, but I would be a liar if I said that I was entirely objective in this. Remembering Orange's description of how shadows and nightmare patterns covered the wall in Dom's room, arms flailing, burn marks from the ropes Orange bound him with dark against his skin, I can't help but feel something I can't quite name. Vindication, perhaps.

Orange said he saw a liquid shine glistening on Dom's hands and arms, and when the light shifted as he walked in, something on Dom's thumbnail, jagged and blue, winked in the light. Orange's gaze went to Dom's face, and then, Orange said, he began to scream.

Sightlessly, Dom screamed back.

I didn't laugh when Orange told me this, but the moon did.

**

At some point, I misplaced my draft notes. Maybe I mis-filed them, or perhaps burned them. Some nights are harder to find than others, and the moon is jealous of my memories. The only piece of them I found was a sheet that had fallen behind the thermal cycler, which I found shortly after injecting the first test drop in the wild. I'd tossed my lab coat aside returning from the café, and it fell to the floor. When I went to pick it up, I saw this:

Despite early indications to the contrary, the agent has not mutated into an airborne form. Secondary infection patterns appear unlikely, but further research is warranted. The agent may potentially be spread through sexual contact, but the window of opportunity is statistically insignificant due to the rapid propagation rate.

**

How exactly did my work spread out? I could imagine a number of ways, but imagining is unnecessary. Juliana knows. She saw it all.

In an alleyway of rats, a woman plunged another needle into her scarred arm.

A few blocks away, a prostitute removed a vial from a leather case. A john sat next to her on the bed, naked and twitching, waiting.

Sitting in a cozy brownstone living room, a man held a syringe up to his window. Billy Holiday crooned to him from his iPod, as he thought of broken hearts and gray tomorrows.

Through the water, I touched them all.

**

Blood around the man's nose and mouth, rusty against pale skin, eyes slack after his last convulsions. I must have seen him die and missed it, I thought as I counted the corpse's needle marks. Pulling the sheet up over the body, I continued checking ER charts, my old residency ID saving me from scrutiny. Most notes are almost illegible, scrawled by whoever was free.

Psychotic episode. Hallucinations. Massive adrenaline shock. Self-inflicted hammer wounds. Self-mutilation, optical. Self-mutilation, genital. Ran in front of city bus.

Behind me, the slam of a gurney on double doors announced another arrival. I did a quick tally as I watched the bleary-eyed paramedics rush through a screaming bloody bundle. Forty-three so far, and in under 24 hours. Unbelievable. I'd vastly underestimated the potentially affected population size.

I walked out into the street. After three different emergency rooms, I estimated my project was averaging a 65 percent fatality rate. Overhead, Juliana stared blankly down, watching me. Now, forever.

The next phase, I promised the moon that still wears her face, will be better.

Ripples

Load sequence.

Begin. Clutch the armrests as the world catches flame.

Atmosphere, friction-fired and seething, pounds against metal and ceramic. Dragons of heat and pressure roar as the nearly abandoned machine tumbles. Klaxons blare.

Strapped into a command couch, the woman clutches her console, white-knuckled. Her left hand presses toggles and buttons. The commander's voice, steady as possible given the circumstances, is swallowed by the ambient noise. She leans in, requests the angle of entry. Current velocity. Estimated point of impact. Expected death toll.

Bone white against sea blue, text scrolls across the console screen. From this vantage point, the words are illegible, swallowed in the chaos of approach.

"Damn," she says, like every time.

The historical record is clear. This is when Commander Siobhan McKenna first knew her death was inexorably upon her. As she stares at the screen, calculating what options are left to her, the station's atmosphere shimmers, a curtain of potentiality rippling in time.

Hold sequence. Watch the commander's face, eyes wide, reflecting re-entry's light from the screens and the small hatch window. Wonder what she was thinking in this eternal now, more than a century behind the instant now. There's no way to truly know. Commander McKenna has less than six minutes left to live.

Start again. Wonder if the blast-furnace howl is as loud to the others, observing Commander McKenna's last heroic moments from behind their own temporal curtains. Ripples in the stream, a lonely death made public history, all but her last few seconds. Check the upgraded software, the level of field control and power modulation. Maybe this time.

Other screens appear, hyperlinks to the sensory inputs hovering into view. A complete breakdown of the orbital mechanics of the station's last day, including the last-minute course correction that killed McKenna but spared Jakarta. The international memorials, the parades, the national holiday in the commander's name. Full text and audio of the speech given by McKenna's only child on the 50th anniversary of her death, honoring her as a mother, crediting her with his decision to go into the astronaut corps.

Lean forward as the light shifts. Last stage of atmospheric insertion starts here. Less than three minutes now, hardly enough time for a song. Not for the first time, wonder what she's thinking now, as she coaxes, swears, bullies the attitude jets into line. Just enough delta-v, just enough time. Her main screen shows potential paths and angles of displacement in lines of calming green and blue.

McKenna slumps back, face drawn. Saving millions must be exhausting. If only she could know the future she would bring, what her sacrifice would mean to the world. Gratitude leading to dialogues leading to real progress, and hope. Imagine that all the others watching, for whatever reason, feel the same.

A soft chime sounds from the armrest, just above the temporal control panel. There are an unprecedented number of observers at this moment in time. So many for whom full sensory recording is insufficient, who need to sense history's progress through the gauze of a chronodynamic field. Reach out a hand to the field, shimmering just before the bank of screens. It tickles, like carbonation against the skin. Feel the field pulse and thrum, a bubble of soap and static.

Think *If I push hard enough, will I fall into this moment? Will I join her? Will I take her place?*

Pull away from the screen, ashamed of the fear flickering through. A chronodynamic field is stable and locked to its point of origin; nobody can fall through one, or even push through. Only information can be collected; no communication, no tangible transference. Even so.

Touch the field again, resting against history's pop and fizz. If communication was possible, what could be said? What might be of use to Commander McKenna as she plunges earthward in a burning hulk? Think *What would I want to hear?*

Lean forward again, close enough now to almost feel the charge on your face. She will never hear, never know what you say, this hero dead decades before your parents' birth. Here, now, for reasons not quite articulate, it seems important to say it anyway.

Tell her she is not alone. Thank her for her death, her willingness to give up everything, literally everything that she is and will be. Knowing she can never hear the words makes the gesture irrelevant, but no less necessary.

Turbulence shakes the burning station, and the last of Commander McKenna's screens die with a burst of sparks and smoke. She slumps back in the seat, exhausted. In these moments, it always seems as if she should look sad, or frightened, but she doesn't. With her remaining life measured in seconds, McKenna is almost smiling. Her expression says *Can you believe this crap?*

"Out of fuel, anyway," she says. "Should've gassed up before I left."

Laugh, even though this scene has played on your consoles innumerable times. The faint warping of chronodynamic fields grows into a ripple, their visual distortion lost in the growing heat shimmers. In 19 seconds, the fatal hull breach—caused by a failed heat shield tile in a recycled ISS module, itself recycled from an ESA crew capsule—will happen. McKenna's death is swift and, for those ghoulish enough to watch the last moments available for normal chronometric viewing, fairly merciful. By all reports, she does not suffer.

Without the attitude jets to correct, the station begins to tumble uncontrollably. McKenna closes her eyes. Fight the urge to do the same as the control room spins and shakes. Focus in on McKenna's face; there is nothing more to learn in the graceless, burning fall of the station.

Four seconds before the end, McKenna smiles one last time. She opens her mouth to speak. Filter out the roar of friction, the shrieking of metal. There's no filtering the pulse in your ears.

"I am not alone," Commander McKenna says.

The world dissolves into flame and thunder. Untold visitors watch though ripples of time, and ponder.

End sequence.

Persistence of Memory

ENWOMBED IN THE drop capsule, Lieutenant 15-Thorne sat nervously, thinking of war. Despite the gelatinous g-couch surrounding him and the heavy battle armor he wore, the sounds of the troop carrier rumbling through the ionosphere came through, the bass vibrations explicating the events outside. Klaxons alternated with the dull thud of capsules shooting through tubes, whooshing into space like spores. A seeding of fire. 15-Thorne shivered at the image.

"Squad leaders, report," the mechanized voice of Captain 7-Smith echoed in his helmet. Beneath him, the rumbling changed pitch, whining higher as the treads pulled his capsule into deploy position. He knew that ten other capsules were syncing into their respective tubes in time with his. Sweat beaded above his eyes, dripping into his eyebrows, making them itch.

"Blue squad is go," he heard himself say, his training speaking through him. His eyes moved to a screen of his imagining, even though the heads-up printed directly on his retinal filaments. Every name showed green, 10 men and women under his command, ready to fall at terminal velocity. "All units in the pipe."

"Roger, blue squad is go," the toneless voice replied. "Stand by for insertion."

The oxygen readout in his right eye blipped, and he consciously slowed his breathing. Deep breath, in and hold, now out. Every drop seemed to take about 10 minutes between insertion warning and the first clutch of gravity. He'd said as much once to the staff sergeant, climbing out of a capsule on a readiness drill. The noncom had barked, as close to a laugh as Sergeant 8-Paul ever got.

"I counted once on my telltale," the sergeant said, before walking off to the mess. "It's seven seconds exactly. Count for yourself next time you drop."

His eyes flicked downward as the digital timer hit 00:07. A sharp shake, and his stomach seemed to climb up into his nose. The first few seconds were smooth and silent as they pierced space's edge dropping down into the gravity well. Through the mimetic alloy skin of the capsule, a rising whistle could be felt, climbing the scale in time with the slow deformation of the outer skin, designed to act as a brake. 15-Thorne visualized the upper end of the capsule bulging out under wind and heat pressure, gradually flowing up and changing shape into a mushroom. It wouldn't quite slow him down to parachute speed, but with a g-couch, that didn't really matter. A brief wobble accelerated his heart rate, and smoothed itself out within a few seconds. Every capsule did that. At least the last 11 he'd dropped in did.

His jaw worked, and the monitor screen inhabited his eye again. All were nominal for hot drops: stress levels moderate, high levels of adrenaline and serotonin. Nobody hyperventilating this trip. For the hundredth time since his promotion to lieutenant in this generation, he wished he could see where he was falling from his perspective, instead of having to tap into the survey line. Looking at a picture taken 15 miles up from a pilotless bird was not nearly the same experience as watching out a window. He brought up the feed anyway.

A swarm of gnats sprang to life in his heads-up. Thousands of capsules falling toward the planet Vestibule, 10 at a time, covering the planet view below in dots of blue-gray smart metal. The sight was beautiful, and horrifying. Falling en masse toward the enemy had never struck him as a fun idea. Maybe the original Elias Thorne had a choice in the matter, but none of his successors did. Or would.

Watching the telltales of his crew, he wondered if their progenitors were still in the service, or even still alive. He would never know, of course; that was forbidden to the point of being a cardinal sin. The price for their service. They got to live as eternal servants of the military machine, while the originals, who had volunteered in the first place, either died or were eventually retired and displaced into civilian life. What irony.

"Lieutenant 15-Thorne, your squad is approaching touchdown. Prepare for E & E."

"Affirmative, Base. Preparing for egress." The telltales were starting to blip up now, the squad ramping for combat. Around each of them, the capsule's g-couch was flowing into a new position, designed for maximum cushioning while allowing a soldier to emerge from the capsule's wreckage ready to fight. The capsule's nose, designed to collapse and absorb the initial shock, was also deploying its own version of the g-couch. *Pretty busy in here*, 15-Thorne thought as he automatically ran through his status checks.

"All checks green, Base. Blue squad ready."

"Affirmative, Lieutenant. Touchdown in 5...4...3...2...1." A loud, jarring thump, followed by the abrupt grasp of gravity and the sound of liquid foam sacs rupturing under pressure. He felt the push downward, but suffered no discomfort; the capsule had done its wonders again. With a small explosive pop, the sides of the capsule fell away, and Lieutenant 15-Thorne leapt from the remains of his ride to the surface of Vestibule.

"Blue squad, sound off," he barked as he ran for the predetermined meeting place, a copse of native trees about thirty meters east of his landing site. Other capsules were still falling, winking brightly in the afternoon sun, but none close to his position. They'd drawn outer flank position this go-round; maybe next time they'd get center fire position.

"12-Johnson, go." The other names in his squad rang in his ears, all affirmative for landing hot and ready. A GPS topo popped into view, gold waves superimposed on the icy dots of his people, pointing towards the battle's heat. Other squads hove into the display, a dissonance of chromatic forces arrayed to the northeast. Their orders were clear in their terms and implications: run flanking action, mop up whoever got missed by the first units, pound the ground and anyone not under it.

Using hand gestures older than the colony worlds most came from, 15-Thorne ordered his team out. They formed up into a triple column and walked north. The lieutenant kept one eye scanning the countryside, whipblade trees green and slender in the chilly aquamarine sky, bright against the muddy Yangtze grass, and one eye monitoring the multiple telltales in his view. Thus, he knew who it was that approached his crew from the west before the soldier came into view. Combat training, drilled in until it reached his core, kept him from reacting.

"Report, Private, and make it quick," he ordered. The private snapped off a quick salute, then fell into step with the lieutenant, rearranging his gear as he talked. On his shoulder, a sleek black pulse gun hung, fat with metal shards and electromagnetic force.

"Private 11-Gomez, sir, with Tac Squad Green-3. My capsule didn't mushroom right, and I ended up nearly a klick south of where I should be. My CO said to hook up with the nearest group and follow them in until I can meet up with my squad. Sir."

"All right, private. Fall into formation at the rear; you can cover us with that streetsweeper you're packing."

The private nodded. "Yes, sir."

"One more thing, private."

11-Gomez turned back. "What's that, sir?"

15-Thorne nodded toward the point of the formation. "One of your clone-brothers is up there. 13th generation. Be careful while you're with us."

The private nodded once. His Adam's apple bulged tight against his throat, then subsided. "Yes, sir." He turned and jogged to the back of the column.

Damn it, 15-Thorne thought as they moved north. Mixing generations in a unit wasn't illegal, but it was a poor idea. Clones of the same person didn't get along, especially in a combat group. Disagreements turned into fights, and fights turned into infirmary trips. More squads had been killed by clone-sibling distractions than direct enemy attack during the first 50 years of clone soldier deployments. Everybody had their own theories as to why clone-siblings couldn't serve together, but 15-Thorne had long since reached a conclusion of his own: They always saw what they disliked most about themselves in each other. It made as much sense as anything official. Who can hate you more than you?

* * *

No matter how many times 15-Thorne dropped, first contact with enemy fire always happened sooner than anticipated. Blue Squad was still three klicks from the main body when a sniper's EM round streaked through the trees, tearing through the late afternoon at a sizable fraction of c. Despite its speed, it made almost no sound, apart from a thin sizzling that could be mistaken for wind. 15-Thorne had barely noticed its light before the projectile struck Private 9-Olafsen high on the left side, brutally tearing the arm from his body and hurling the body backwards several yards, spinning as it fell.

"Sniper!" Blue Squad was down in the long grass before the cry finished its echo, lying low and trying to track the source of the fire. The sniper fired again, severing a sproutling tree neatly in two. *Idiot*, 15-Thorne thought, hearing the whine of long-range rifles powering up in the breeze.

"Private 4-Thomas here, sir. I have a track," a husky female voice said in his ear. The lieutenant nodded; she was one of his best shooters. Telltale clicks on the subvocal channels came in, indicating two others had tracks as well. The coordinates came in just then, adjusted by GPS to compensate for everyone's position.

"Fire at will," 15-Thorne said.

The world caught flame. Several crossing beams of light, the EM projectiles tearing up the sky as they left their signs of fire and force, arrowed from the tall grass into the trees. The susurration of so many rounds sounded like a chorus of cicadas whispering, broken only by the cracking of branches and the wet slap of something high dying quickly. 15-Thorne nodded; what remaining pieces were small, and fell before they could be ID'd.

"Give me a look-see, 4T," he said.

A stand of green-yellow weedlike growths shook briskly for a moment. That was her acknowledgement, 15-Thorne knew, because he couldn't see anything else moving. 00:24 was the count when her voice came back on. "Definitely a Vestibule militiaman, sir. There's just about enough left to pick out the colors."

"Acknowledged. Get back and give Johnson a hand with Ole. We'll prep for meat wagon evac before we move on."

"Yes, sir," he heard. *I don't like it either*, he wanted to say.

Ole had been a good soldier and friend to many in his battal-ion. He would be again, but not to the soldiers of Blue Squad, 103rd Battalion. Some other battalion, a few months from now, would welcome Private 10-Olafson into their ranks, his mem-ory as complete as the meat wagons could make it. That was fair; on their next duty cycle out, they too would welcome someone else's returning dead into the fold.

In his ear, 4T's voice clicked on. "Sir, Ole is tagged and bagged, casualty beacon active."

"Good. We're moving on." He chinned the all-squad chan-nel. "Move out, troops."

The column moved on. 15-Thorne spared only one brief glance at 9-Olafson as he passed, the bloody means of his death disguised in a dark polymer shroud marked clearly with the Pan-Humana Conference medical insignia. Everyone in the squad was an old hand at corpse prep duties by now: he didn't bother checking whether 4T had picked up Ole's tags. She'd hand them over at camp.

"Lieutenant, we've got movement up ahead," 13-Gomez reported from point. 15-Thorne's eyes flicked back to the new one, then forward again. *Thank God telltales don't pick up facial heat*, he thought.

"Where, Gomez?"

Silence for a moment. 15-Thorne could almost hear the thoughts completing in Gomez's head. None of the grunts had the same level of GPS info that he did, but they had enough. If the lieutenant wasn't seeing them…

"Uh, about sixty meters ahead. They're in the brush, about ten meters east of our position. I can't see what they're doing, but if someone were to set up a textbook ambush on this road, these folks would have to scoot over."

"Gomez, take Werner and loop east. See how close you

can get and give me a better idea who it is. They may just be throwing a tea party."

"Yes, sir. I'll be sure to ask."

"Be polite now."

"Like the Corps taught me, sir. Out." Two blips went into standby in 15-Thorne's display, and he forced himself to keep breathing regularly. Command decisions in combat may result in fatalities, the training told him. He recalled those words whenever he sent troops out into potentially dangerous situations. Thin comfort, every time.

The subvocal clicked on.

"Move up behind point, sir?"

15-Thorne almost chuckled. 4T, always in a hurry.

His chin switch moved. "Hold position until point calls in."

"Affirmative."

He imagined the look on her face, held in a laugh. His youngest sister used to look like that when—

Damn it, he thought, squeezing his eyes shut and shaking his head. *Not my memories. Never were. This is all the family I have. All I'll ever have.*

The panic light went off in his eyes, glaring terminal red through his eyelids. GPS info flowered into multiple layers of light, and the vocal channel blasted into life, a heartbeat before the sound of older chemical weapons chattered from the position ahead.

"Sir, it's a fucking bullet party here. We're pinned by two squads with retrofitted mini-guns, and it looks like they've got some mortars, too. We need immediate backup."

"Got it, Gomez. Do what you can." He chinned the panic signal and hit the all-talk circuit. "Light 'em up, troops. 4T, take Li and Johnson and head around west. Everybody else, move forward. Gomez, give me some more info."

No reply. In his readout, the blip for Gomez began to blink yellow.

Shit.

Now Werner's blip was blinking, too.

"Move up. 11-Gomez!"

"Sir?"

"Pull out your sweeper. You and I are going in first."

"Yes, sir." The whine of a microfusion engine seeped onto the circuit, and to Thorne's surprise, the overall display wavered a bit before the hard circuits kicked in.

"11-Gomez, have you modified your weapon?"

The hesitation in the private's voice said it all. "Wasn't getting the proper action, sir. Thought I could get it fixed myself; you know how the quartermaster is with these guns."

"I do, Private. If the EM readings are right, I might be grateful."

They took the lead position and crept forward carefully, the sounds of bullets flying growing to a roar just ahead. Over a small rise in the path, Thorne could see the light of an EM round in the late afternoon sky. The Vestibule militia, except for the occasional sniper, didn't have EM weapons yet, but lead was lead: good for killing, and had been for centuries, at any speed.

"Ready, Private?"

Bass rumble from the pulse rifle, as a cloud of metal shards slipped into the chamber.

"Ready, sir."

Lieutenant 15-Thorne raised his EM rifle to his shoulder, slipped the catch to full automatic, offered a brief prayer to a god whose name he couldn't remember.

"Fire."

The pulse rifle made a coughing sound to Thorne's right,

and the closest militiaman to their position disappeared in a cloud of red mist, billowing over the ambusher's position like a poison fog. Thorne had heard about the pulse rifle's effect on people, but had never seen one up close.

Jesus Christ, he thought.

A young woman, dressed in militia colors and wearing a Pan-Humana flak jacket, turned toward the cloud and saw them crouched behind the rise. Her weapon was almost in position when Thorne shot her, a poisoned stream flowing from his weapon's muzzle. Behind her, the mortars were turning their way, but too slowly. Like watering a lawn, he sprayed their position with relativistic fire, as the pulse rifle coughed again and again. From the west, a lancing of fire erupted as 4T and her fellows opened up. Behind them, the rest of Blue Squad spread out along the perimeter, looking for stragglers and reinforcements.

Out of habit, the digital readout was counting off in the upper corner of Thorne's eye, from the time he and 11-Gomez first opened fire. As the last shuddering from the militiamen ceased and the EM guns wound down, Thorne looked to see the count reach 00:15. A textbook attack, if a little slow.

Tempus fugit, Thorne thought as his squad began tending their wounded and checking for enemy survivors. The wounded were limited to 13-Gomez and 7-Werner, but both were seriously hurt. Werner had been shot twice, Gomez three times.

"Give me the news, Private," Thorne said, examining Werner's shattered leg. Blood oozed slowly from the pressure splint, but he could see clotting around the edge of the bandage. He figured Werner would live, at least for a while.

"Werner's got a busted leg, and probably a cracked rib, but he's stable for now. Gomez isn't going to make it, though. He took two to the chest, and it sounds like one nicked his lung.

Maybe 20 minutes, and he'll drown." 4-Li finished wrapping a cut on Werner's forearm and stood up, not meeting Thorne's eyes. "He's not hurting. That's all I got, sir."

"It'll have to do, Private. Thanks." Thorne chinned the all-talk line, gave the order to fall in and keep moving. Bivouac was at least an hour ahead, and only idiots or loonies wanted to be alone on an enemy world at night. The column formed up, Werner propping himself up on a salvaged Vestibule rifle as he hobbled along behind 4T. No one watched as Thorne crouched beside 13-Gomez's body, his hands clenching themselves as he spoke.

"Private, you're prepped for evac, but we both know that the wagon won't be along for a couple of hours. You've got a choice here. I'll help you if you want it." He held up a silver capsule, breakaway leaves along the side marking it as a field syringe. "Know what this is?"

13-Gomez nodded, his eyes calm. "Some kind of bio-refrigerant, right?"

"That's it. Five minutes after injection, it spreads through your brain and freezes your neurons tight. Preserves the brain better for recovery. It'll stop a thought in mid-sentence, they tell me. It's got to go in before brain death, though, or it's pointless. I'd have used it on Ole if I'd had the chance; it's a shame to have to go all the way back to baseline copy."

"Yeah." 13-Gomez closed his eyes. "Sir?"

"Yes?"

"I've got a better idea. Why don't you borrow 11-Gomez's pulse rifle for a moment, put the muzzle under my chin and erase me?"

15-Thorne sat back on his heels. His face turned red.

"Come on, sir. You're a 15th generation copy. How many years are you carting around in your head? How many combat drops, how many weeks of drills? And most of them aren't yours." 13-Gomez gasped, clenched his teeth, relaxed. "I counted mine up once. I figure I've got roughly 112 years of military life in here," he tapped the side of his head, "only three of which are mine."

15-Thorne nodded. "Mine is 141, five and a half this generation."

"You see? You're a five year old body dragging around nearly a century and a half of someone else's thoughts. Your memories, your instincts: none of that is yours. The person they belonged to died decades ago. Same as me, same as all of us." He coughed, pink froth spraying from his lips. "I don't want to be that anymore, sir."

"Gomez, you know they'll just keep cloning you. There'll be a fresh one force-grown and out of the tanks in a couple of weeks, if there isn't one in waiting now."

"Yeah. Hell, you've already got a spare, don't you? But, all the ones after me will start from baseline, unless 11-Gomez there survives long enough to make a new one, and I doubt he will. Pulsers tend to go out as vapor." He spat a bright red globule onto the ground. "I remember."

"What good will it do to make them start from zero?"

"I don't know, sir. Maybe they'll be all right with it for a while, maybe it'll never bother them. Hell, it wasn't 'til about six months ago it started to bug me."

Thorne sighed, his body suddenly heavy in the dying afternoon light. It wasn't the first time he'd heard this request. It was illegal to do, illegal to consider; hell, it was illegal just to ask. Lots of laws broken in one sentence, and not one of them meant a damn. Maybe the originals never thought about it, the purgatory they were condemning themselves to over and over again. Or maybe they did, and thought it was just.

"Sir?"

"Private, you know that Pan-Humana military law forbids such a request. Under the circumstances, however, a report need not be made; you're obviously in extreme circumstances."

13-Gomez sighed. "Yes, sir. Thank you, sir."

15-Thorne continued, as if Gomez hadn't spoken. "Per regulations, I have tagged you for casualty retrieval, which makes you exempt from further combatant status. Our status on this mission calls your chances for peaceful retrieval into question, however." The lieutenant spoke clearly and formally, like a witness testifying before the court. "Private Alvario 13-Gomez, are you carrying a sidearm?"

The private frowned. Surely the lieutenant knew that he wasn't; sidearms weren't considered standard issue for ground infantry. "No, sir."

"Ah. Then, in light of our present status, I am assigning you the use of mine until evacuation." In one smooth motion, Lieutenant 15-Thorne pulled the .50 Peacemaker Rex handgun from its hip holster and handed it, grip first, to 13-Gomez. "I will expect the return of this weapon at earliest opportunity, Private."

Through the gathering of foam on his lips, 13-Gomez smiled.

"Yes, sir."

"Excellent." Thorne saluted, his eyes unreadable under the sudden shade. "Until the next drop, Private."

"Next drop, sir."

15-Thorne stood there, holding the salute for just a second longer than protocol demanded, saying goodbye. He turned on his heel and marched toward bivouac double-time to catch his squad. When the shot came, he pretended not to hear it and kept marching.

Giuseppe's Boughs

WHEN THE CAR EMERGED into Hell, the first thing Giuseppe Banca did was squint. Sunshine, strong and warm, shone from a pale yellow sky. Hell's landscape was a rolling sea of grass and purple-tinged trees, stretching over slight rises and falls for what looked like forever. There was no curve to the world Giuseppe could see.

"Not what you expected," the driver said. A handsome face glanced at Giuseppe from the rearview, gold-and-grey eyes twinkling.

"No," Giuseppe said. He wiped a strong, callused hand across his forehead. Frigid air roared from the vents, smelling of machines. It gave Giuseppe a headache. "Could you turn down the air a little?"

"Sorry," the driver said, twisting a dial. "Most visitors think it's hotter than it is."

They drove down a two-lane road, a waist-high spiky basalt wall the only other sign of habitation. No telephone poles, litter or road signs. Giuseppe needed the job, but the unexpected sense of peace he felt looking out over Hell was the first emotion he'd felt this trip other than worry or fear.

At the top of a rise little more than a swelling, a tall figure stood next to a broad tree, covered in shade. The driver drove into a dirt turnaround, parking within feet of the figure, and got out. Giuseppe climbed out of the back seat, straightening his only suit as the two spoke.

"Mr. Banca," the driver called. Giuseppe walked into the shade, forcing himself to relax. As his eyes adjusted, he saw the men were nearly twins; only the eyes were different, the gold-

and-grey of the driver in sharp contrast to the green-and-black of the person he was meeting.

"Beelzebub, Lord of the Flies," the second man said. He bowed his head but did not offer his hand. "You've met Uriel." The driver nodded, and in the dappled sunlight, Giuseppe could see the tattoo running up the angel's forearm: a broadsword, lined in flames and blood.

"Your resume is impressive, Mr. Banca," Beelzebub said. "I assume you see the problem."

Giuseppe looked up at the branches. Many of the leaves were discolored, some completely dead, others spotted with brittle patches. He followed mottled rot down twigs, across branches into the trunk, and into the roots. He walked around the tree, and on the other side at about shoulder-height, found a large milky purple oval growth, like a crystal in the wood.

"I'm not familiar with this type of tree," Giuseppe said.

"It's a soul," Uriel said, amused.

"Souls are a little outside my experience," Giuseppe said slowly.

"Some time ago, all the condemned of Hell began to grow roots," Beelzebub said, his voice taut. "We could not dislodge them once planted, or prevent them from transforming. Within a decade, all the damned were like this."

"Why not let them die?" Giuseppe asked.

"You misunderstand Hell," Uriel said gently.

"It is not willed where what is willed must be," Beelzebub said. "Our duty is to maintain these... ephemera in damnation, on pain of intervention," Beelzebub sharply gestured at Uriel, "but growing things is not among our skills."

Giuseppe walked around the tree again, re-examining everything. He took a piece of paper from his pocket, brushed his hand against the trunk and leaves onto the paper, and smeared his hand across the sheet. He carefully questioned Beelzebub on water and nutrients. He looked closely at the shape and direction of the dead spots, mottling of the bark and direction of the leaves' curling.

Finally, Giuseppe reached out and gently touched the crystalline growth. Floods of images and sensations roared through him, leaving the taste of oil and smoke. He saw an entire life in seconds, years of despair and the eventual spiral downward. A name floated up in the whirlwind of his brain—the soul trapped inside whose damnation hardened into bark and leaf, growing into a sickness that failed to belong, even here—and sank away as Giuseppe pulled back.

He looked at the demon and the angel, his gaze falling to the tattoo on Uriel's arm. An idea struck him; its audacity, in this place of torment that seemed anything but, emboldened him.

"May I?" Giuseppe asked.

Uriel followed Giuseppe's gaze. A broad grin escaped him. "No human has; you might as well be the first." The guardian of Eden put his hand over the tattoo and drew a weapon of fire from his arm, flame and steel bright in the sun. Carefully, he handed the sword to Giuseppe, hilt first.

Giuseppe took the sword, chill to the touch and nearly weightless. He turned to the tree whose name he now knew, gripped the hilt with both hands, and swung at a point just above the ensouled knot, knowledge of the sword's effect somehow forming before he swung. At the sword's touch, the upper trunk and branches dissipated into dust, swirling in the sword's wake before fading to nothing. The trunk stood bare, the cut exposing dark inner wood that glistened in the sun.

He swung vertically twice more, then downward at an angle below the knot. As the dust scattered, only the growth was left, lying next to a mulchy hole in the ground. Handing the sword back to Uriel, Giuseppe got down on his knees and dug out handfuls of mud and loam. Carefully, he buried the crystalline knot, loosely packing in the dirt. Stillness settled over the rough mound, and Giuseppe was struck by how right the rich dirt felt beneath his hands. He sat back and looked at the mound, understanding in some part of his heart beyond the reach of reason or faith that it would in time grow again into a tree, but healthy and right.

A shadow passed over him, and the low buzzing of insects.

"Huh," Beelzebub said. Behind him, Uriel smiled, and touched his eyebrow in salute.

Surrounded by the sunlit work of lifetimes, Giuseppe Banca looked at those who brought him here, and laughed joyously.

About the Author

Brandon Nolta is a writer, editor, and professional curmudgeon living in the transportation-challenged wilds of north Idaho. After earning an MFA, he went slightly mad. Nothing much happened with that, so he gave it up and started working for respectable companies again, which he still does when he's not pounding away at the keyboard to the sweet strains of Miles Davis and the occasional burst of EDM. His fiction and poetry have appeared in *Stupefying Stories, The Pedestal Magazine, Every Day Fiction, Uncanny Magazine,* and a cacophony of other publications. *Iron and Smoke,* published by Montag Press in 2015, was his first book; *These Shadowed Stars,* a collection of the short fiction he has published over the last 20 years, is his second.

www.ingramcontent.com/pod-product-compliance
Lightning Source LLC
Chambersburg PA
CBHW030251270626
47156CB00021B/1644